Mia stared down at herself and watched as a tear splashed into the sea. Just one tear, sending a shimmer across her reflection. When the tiny ripple smoothed away, the face was different – wider across the cheekbones, the eyes suddenly huge and dark. Mia blinked, thinking that more tears were blurring her sight, but when she looked again, the features were even clearer, and she could see a swirl of dark reddish hair floating around the face.

It wasn't her reflection. There was another girl gazing at her out of the water, frowning at Mia, biting her lip anxiously as she broke the surface.

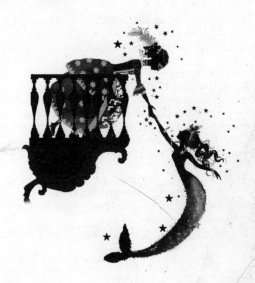

Holly Webb

The Mermaid's Sister

ORCHARD

ORCHARD BOOKS

First published in Great Britain in 2016 by The Watts Publishing Group

7 9 10 8 6

Text copyright © Holly Webb, 2016

A CIP catalogue record for this book
is available from the British Library.

ISBN 978 1 40832 764 7

Typeset in Adobe Caslon by
Avon DataSet Ltd, Bidford-on-Avon, Warwickshire
Printed and bound in Great Britain by
CPI Group (UK) Ltd, Croydon, CR0 4YY

The paper and board used in this book are
made from wood from responsible sources.

Orchard Books
An imprint of
Hachette Children's Group
Part of The Watts Publishing Group Limited
Carmelite House
50 Victoria Embankment
London EC4Y 0DZ

An Hachette UK Company
www.hachette.co.uk

www.hachettechildrens.co.uk

For Tom, Robin
and William

MIA WATCHED AS THEY walked away from her, the golden embroidery on her mother's dress glinting in the low morning sunlight. She didn't understand where Mama and her elder brother were going, or why her mother had stroked her cheek and wound her fingers so tightly in Mia's hair. Mia had traced her fingers over the embroidery again, and rubbed her face against its beautiful roughness.

They were far away now, making for a boat pulled up at the jetty, a dark-cloaked soldier standing by to hand them in. Mama was leaning on Zuan as though she was too tired to walk, and his head was hanging. A sudden panic seemed to rise up inside Mia, and she took one stumbling step forward, before she was caught and held on the palace steps.

The glittering threads of the embroidery pulled at Mia, tugging at something deep inside. Then they stretched, thinner and thinner – almost too slight and delicate to see, but still there, wrapped around her heart.

'Stay here with me, Mia,' her cousin Olivia murmured, wrapping Mia in her arms. 'You can't go with them, I'm so sorry.'

'Mama...' Mia whispered.

But her mama didn't look back, and the boat crept away across the shining water of the lagoon, swallowed up into the white sunlight.

CHAPTER ONE

MIA DREAMED, AND THE COLD green water swirled around her, around and over, deep and dark. When she'd been little, the white and gold and silver horses had taken her riding through the floods. She had laughed and screamed in childish joy as she raced with the waves, digging her heels into Lorin's glimmering sides, begging the silver mare to gallop faster.

But even then, when she had still let herself play in the water, she had never seen the sea like this.

This sea was only for her dreams, the journeys she made in the deep dark of the night.

She scooped her arms through the water, slow and sleepy, feeling the delicious shiver as the silky cold brushed over her skin. Mia swam down deeper, slipping between the heavy ribbons of black weed. The sunlight from the surface was fading now, just a faint whitish bloom along the top of the water. Bubbles trailed up past her like a silver necklace, and she twisted lazily to watch them go.

A pale hand dabbed at a bubble, and Mia laughed. She hadn't seen them! She'd been looking so hard! But now they were all around her, their tails flickering in the dimness.

She stretched out her hands to them and saw them smile and reach for her. Mia smiled. She knew this game – she reached further, launching herself through the water, slow and heavy compared to the mergirls with their jewelled tails. Always they whisked away from her at the last moment. It had made her so cross, when she was smaller!

A clear image of herself as a little girl – a true memory rather than a dream – flashed behind her eyes, and Mia halted, blinking, the seawater suddenly stinging her eyes. She was dreaming *now* – she knew she must be, even though the sea felt so real. Surely one didn't have memories in dreams? Then the chill of the deep sea washed over her again, and as more memories rose around her Mia forgot how strange it was to *know* she dreamed.

She remembered herself, so small. A tiny child, left behind on the fine white sand of the sea bed, stamping her little feet. She had torn angrily at the waterweeds until her fingers bled from their sharp edges. One of the mermaids had swum back to Mia then, her dark eyes wide and worried, her long swathes of red hair swirling around her face. It was the first time any of them had ever touched her.

The mermaid unwound the weeds with glass-cool fingers, and bound Mia's hands again with different plants, soft and soothing. The mermaid had been older than Mia, but not that much older. Like a sister. Mia remembered her cloud of red hair as she lay cradled against the mergirl's shoulder. The soothing murmur, like the lapping of little ripples. Her hands hadn't even been marked when she woke next morning – but for a day or so there had been a faint stiffness across her fingers, as of a long-healed scar, aching in the cold.

She looked eagerly for the red-haired mergirl now, but they swooped and darted around her so quickly it was impossible to tell them apart. Mia dived after them, but they were too fast for a mortal child with no tail, all wound up in a lace-trimmed nightgown. Instead, she hopped here and there, putting out her hands almost at random, in case she could catch a mermaid by accident. She longed to feel their smooth, chill skin again.

She caught a fingerful of lace-like tail fin – and then it was gone. Two mergirls swung, darting back past her, their hands stretched out to tease. Mia gasped, and reached. But her fingertips brushed theirs, and then they were gone, and she was suddenly, heartbreakingly awake again.

Mia sat up, gasping, and wrapped her arms around her middle. There was a hole inside, where something had been ripped away. If she didn't hold tight, she'd fall apart.

'Come back,' she whispered, peering out into the darkness of her room. In the dream, the light had been shimmering on the water, and it still glittered and burned at the corners of her eyes. But there was no one there now, only shadows.

Mia shook her head. Who was she whispering to? The mergirls dancing in the water? Or her mother and brother, their little boat vanishing into the bright sunshine? She blinked and shuddered, and remembered that she was awake, and she was horribly, desperately alone.

She gasped in a breath, and the golden threads of her mother's embroidered dress sealed up the hole inside her, covering it over with a hard, armoured shell.

Or perhaps a scar, Mia thought sadly, staring down at her fingers, folded on her knees. Could you have a scar, inside? This was a scar that was only half-healed. It stabbed and burned, whenever someone knocked against it.

Sometimes, Mia thought that her dreams were the most real thing about her. They were stronger and brighter than the dim days in the palace, where she had to pretend she couldn't hear the rumours, and they didn't hurt.

She didn't dream every night – it happened more when she was upset. The dreams were a refuge. The deep stillness of the undersea world soothed her, after she'd spent hours at some diplomatic ceremony, enduring the tide of whispers as she stood by Olivia's throne. When she felt lost and alone, the golden ties to her mother made her feel loved again – that she did belong to someone, after all.

The dreams about her family were always the same. She would be standing by the water, as she had been that last time she saw them. Way out across the lagoon she could see a tiny boat, black against the silent water, and so far away that she could never follow after it. She was crying, and calling out, and then the golden threads would appear around her wrists, glittering and fine. She could never tell where they had come from – from somewhere inside her, perhaps? They stretched out across the water, hard to see against the sunny ripples, but strong. They pulled tight.

They hurt, sometimes. She woke up gasping, her wrists pressed against her heart. Once or twice she had even found herself out of bed, pressed up against the window, as though she had been trying to get out and go – where? She didn't know.

She loved the dream, even when it hurt her. Her mother and brother were like characters in a story now. It was a book that belonged only to her, a story that she read to herself in secret – but real, or it had been once. She knew, really, that she would never see them again *except* in dreams. They were in exile, banished from the city for their treachery against her cousin and her uncle. Mia had been left behind, but she felt like an exile too, separated from the rest of the court by the whispers, and the worried way her cousin Olivia sometimes eyed her.

Mia climbed out of bed and pulled open her window shutters, letting in the sharp honey-golden light. So much had changed, since the day her mama had left her there by the water…

She had always missed her mother, of course she had. But even before Mama and Zuan had gone, the Lady Sofia had been so busy with affairs of the court that she hadn't had much time to play with her little daughter – except once or twice, Mia remembered, when she had conjured up some pretty spell.

There had been a golden ball that Mia loved. She remembered clapping her hands in excitement as Mama shaped it in her long, thin hands, and it shone from deep inside, like the sun. The ball had rolled and bounced along the palace corridors, while tiny Mia trotted after it and chuckled.

Mia shivered, and peered through the dim morning light towards the great wooden chest that stood in one corner of her bedroom. The ball was still there, buried in a corner somewhere, under a pile of broken dolls and a sailing boat with tangled rigging. It was dull now, and heavy, and it made her sad to look at it.

Moments of happiness with her mama had been rare, Mia admitted to herself. She was a child of the palace, reared to stand quietly by her mother as she took part in the ceremonies and rituals that were demanded of the royal family. Mostly she remembered her mother as a shining, rustling, scented creature, in one beautiful dress after another – always in the finest fabrics, embroidered with gold. She had spent hours standing by Mama's side, tracing her fingers over the patterns. It was all she remembered from when they took her mother away.

After they'd gone, it was Mia's cousin Olivia, who led the city. Olivia's father was still the duke, but he was so ill, so worn out by a lifetime of magic, that Olivia – not even a teenager – had to rule for him, with her council. But she'd still played with Mia, far more than Mama ever had. Olivia's magic was so strong and so beautiful, and Mia adored her. One day, she too would be able to call the waters and protect the city from the floods, just like her big cousin.

Olivia had been the one to find the creatures in the water again. She had fallen in the canal and been rescued by one of the white and golden horses that had been companions to the people of Venice since the city had been built – although they hadn't known it for so many years. The horse – his name was Lucian – had saved Olivia, and between them he and Olivia had restored the love of magic to the city. It was hard not to believe, not to see the power of the water, when the horses went tumbling up the canals, tossing their manes in excitement as they plunged through the flood waters.

Until Olivia had made the city and the grand old gentlemen of her ruling council see the power of the water horses, the royal family had been trying to control the floods with their magic alone. They had been forcing them back with pure power, instead of channelling the waters and accepting that building a city on marshland meant that occasionally one had to get wet. It was the constant, exhausting use of that power that had finally killed Olivia's father.

Olivia had brought the waters into the palace, deeper in than they had ever been before. A whole new suite of rooms had been created, built right out over the edge of the water, furnished with floating platforms that simply rose up over the floods. It was almost like living on a boat, and it meant that the water horses could be part of her council too. Lucian and several of the other horses slept there, drowsing on the floating platforms, each with one foreleg trailing in the water.

Mia had loved to play there, and Olivia had played with her, laughing as Mia and her favourite horse, the mare Lorin, chased each other through the shallows. Mia was her cousin's darling, she knew it. Only Mia could run into a meeting of the council and seize her cousin's hand and drag her away. Then they'd go splashing in the shallow water that lapped across the marble floors. They could kick up great clouds of spray and watch Lorin and Lucian dance through it after them. Mia and Olivia would lie stretched out along their strong, shining backs and fall asleep, lulled by sunlight on the water. It had been blissful – and when Mia had cried for her mother, Olivia held her, and rocked her, and brushed her tears away.

So although Mia missed her family, she had been happy – so happy. But as she grew older, she began to see that there was something in the way that Olivia's councillors and the other members of the court looked at her. A watchful wariness that she didn't understand.

'Why doesn't she like me?' she'd whispered once to Olivia, after one of the ladies-in-waiting twitched away the figured silk of her skirt. Mia had only wanted to stroke the pattern – something in the twisted threads reminded her of her mother.

'Oh, Mia. She does. Perhaps she didn't want you

to mark the silk,' her cousin murmured, smiling. 'Look at your dirty fingers!'

Mia had nodded, but she wasn't sure that Olivia was right. She wasn't sure that Olivia even believed that herself. And it went on – years of whispers, and sideways looks, and turning away.

It was a statue that explained it, in the end. Her cousin, on a stone plinth in the piazza, looking out over the water where Mia's mother and brother had disappeared. Her face was hard and gleaming in bronze, and her enamelled eyes glittered. There were other statues of Olivia and portraits too, with softer, sweeter gazes. But to Mia now, that hard, bronze face was the one that seemed the most like her – now she knew what her cousin had done.

The inscription read: *Her Most Serene Highness, Lady Olivia, with gratitude, on the occasion of the banishment of the usurper.*

Mia had walked past it for years, only smiling at her cousin's fussy hairstyle and the way there always seemed to be a huge seagull sitting on her shoulder.

The statue was spelled not to let them land, but the seagulls didn't care. They ate everything, and Mia suspected they had simply eaten the spell.

Mia was seven, only a few years younger than Olivia had been when the statue was made. She had been reading court documents with her tutors, and now she stopped and read the inscription properly for the first time. 'What's a usurper?' she asked her lady-in-waiting, as they passed the statue. 'And what did Cousin Olivia do to him?'

The lady-in-waiting was a dim, pretty girl from a good family, and she didn't know what to say. She stuttered something, and tried to hurry Mia away, but Mia stood her ground, even more determined now.

'Well? What does it mean?' She looked the statue up and down, and her cousin's stubborn, serious face glared back at her under those silly curls.

'A usurper is someone who steals the throne, Lady Mia,' the lady-in-waiting whispered at last.

'And Olivia stopped them?'

'Yes, my lady.'

'Oh…' Why would that make the girl blush and stammer so? Mia frowned, and then the whispering and indrawn breaths she had heard for so long seemed to shift and settle again inside her head.

Poor child…

I'm amazed the duchess was gracious enough to let her stay! For all they say she was too young to know, she was bewitched by her mother, wasn't she?

Who knows when she might decide to betray her cousin?

Bad blood, it always comes out.

With the hurt anger of a seven-year-old, Mia ran straight to her cousin, begging to be told that it wasn't true. That it was a mistake – Olivia hadn't sent her mother away.

Her cousin swept her up, abandoning the council meeting that Mia had burst into and hurrying her down to the rooms on the water. They'd sat there together for ages, staring out at the sea, both of them with faces streaked by tears.

'How could you?' Mia whispered. 'You sent her away! I miss her so much, and I know nothing about them! I don't even know if they're still alive!'

'Mia, she was plotting against me and my father. She wanted me to marry Zuan, so she could rule through us both.'

'Maybe she just thought you'd love him!' Mia argued. She hardly remembered her brother – only as a tall, angry presence in her mother's rooms. 'I don't believe you! I won't!'

But why would everyone else believe, if it wasn't true? Perhaps her mother had been a traitor.

'Why didn't you tell me?' she whispered, leaning against Olivia's arm. 'I never knew! That stupid Lady Maria had to explain it to me. I never knew why they went away. I should have asked!'

'I was going to tell you. I wanted to wait until you were a little older and you'd understand more.' Olivia stroked Mia's hair. 'I knew how angry you'd be. I didn't want you to be angry with me, Mia.'

'Everyone knows, don't they?'

'Yes...' Olivia admitted.

'Do you think my mother bewitched me?' Mia shook Olivia's hand away. 'Are you waiting for some bad magic to take me over? Do you really think I'd betray you?' She laughed a little, a sad laugh, but she expected her cousin to hug her and tell her of course not.

Olivia only paused, frowning out at the sea.

'You do!' Mia jumped up, staring at her in horror. 'You think I would...' Then she gasped, and ran back into the palace, splashing blindly through the water, as her eyes burned with tears.

Mia had been almost ready to believe what Olivia and the court said about her mother, although she was sure that it had been exaggerated somehow. That there had been some sort of misunderstanding. But then to find that Olivia suspected she was involved too had cast all that away. Mia *knew* she wasn't a traitor. She had loved and trusted Olivia so deeply, and she had assumed that her cousin trusted her.

Olivia and the water horses, and all the city's magic – it was tainted now for Mia, poisoned by suspicion and hurt and anger. Water now was Olivia's. Water was for the horses, who had made Mia into an outcast. She would *never* allow herself to love the water. She would never let herself see the creatures from the canals, or the deeper, slower, more fascinating things that lived out in the dark lagoon.

From then on Mia's meetings with her cousin were almost silent. Mia seemed to see her through a glittering mist of fury and resentment. Olivia looked hard, like her statue, and they never again danced together, or even touched hands.

When Olivia sent for her, Mia went reluctantly to the water chamber. She would stand in front of her cousin, hating her, and hating the water that she had made her own. Lucian, the greatest of the water horses, would stoop over her and let his silver-white mane trail around her shoulders. Lorin would nuzzle at her plaintively, whispering words of love, pleading with Mia to love her back.

Every time, Mia longed to fling her arms around Lorin's smooth neck and feel the magic and the love reaching out to her from the waters of the city. But she stood still, not even flinching away. She pretended that she couldn't see the horses, and it was the hardest thing she'd ever done.

Then her cousin would sigh, kiss Mia's marble-cold cheek, and send her away.

If Olivia and the horses had seen her dreams – the deep-sea dreams, the ones Mia loved so much but tried so hard to forget – they would know that it was all an act. When she woke up and remembered the glinting water, and the tails swirling in the deep, she hated herself. But in her dreams the horses saw her, and they spoke to her, and Mia suspected angrily that those dreams of the sea were even more real than the golden threads that bound her to her mother. She tried so hard, but she couldn't stop herself dreaming.

She was torn...

Mia leant on the sill now, closing her eyes and feeling the pink glow of the sun through her eyelids. But the sense of the dark water swirling around her limbs lingered, and she could feel the pull of the canal two floors below, the water sparkling in the early-morning sun. It called to her, the silken water folding itself slowly against the stones as a boatman sculled past. The magic in her blood quickened and rose, and Mia crushed it back down. She did no magic. She had no magic. She was nothing – *nothing* – like her stone-hard cousin.

Olivia was so strong, everyone said so. The cleverest water magician there had been in centuries. Her advisor Signor Jac and the others who had been part of his gang were all mages too. Even though they lived on a barge moored out in the lagoon, like poor sailors, they were some of the most powerful people in the city.

Mia *should* be like them – and so without ever really allowing herself to think about it, she had made herself *not*, clutching at the growing magic and squashing it down, burying it deep inside. She sealed it away, so that she could never be cold and cruel like her cousin.

The magic was in her blood – but then as all the whisperers said, so was treachery and deceit. The rest of the court were delighted that she seemed to be growing up with no magic. She was ten years old now, most definitely the age by which her magic should be spilling out of her, causing her to explode with fountains of glittering light, or summon flights of tiny birds to swirl around her in the courtyard.

But there was nothing, and the watchful courtiers dismissed her for a failure – thankfully. Many of the ladies-in-waiting seemed to think that her mother had damaged her, by laying spells upon her as a baby. It was just another thing they whispered about, and Mia tried not to listen. In the dark of the night, though, she wondered if they could be right. There was the niggling memory of her mother's tawny-golden eyes, and that pattern of gold embroidery. What had her mother been doing to her, seven years ago?

Mia tried so hard to deny that her mama was a traitor. It must have been her uncle's fault – Olivia's father. He had been a weak magician, and her mother had been trying to protect the city.

'It wasn't a plot…' she murmured, but her voice was carried away in the splashing of the water below. She had spent the night watching the figures darting in and out of the weed forests. She'd stroked the pearly shells on the sea floor, and felt the fine sand shifting between her toes. The cool depths of the sea had cleared her mind.

It was true. Her mother had wanted to rule. Everything she had done was about seizing power for herself and Zuan.

But Mia had only been a little girl! It had been nothing to do with her! Why did everyone think of her as her mother's daughter still, and not Olivia's cousin?

'But they do,' Mia whispered miserably to

the water. 'They all do. Even *she* does. She doesn't trust me.'

The ripples glittered, and slapped against the stones, and Mia sighed. No one had said anything for a while, or at least she hadn't heard them. That had made yesterday all the harder…

She had been sitting on a stool by Olivia's side, watching as her cousin received the Talish ambassador yet again. His visits were always long, and meant hours of pretty speeches back and forth. Horrible rumours were chasing round the palace, threats of war and talk of the Emperor and his son, and the ambassador looked grander and sleeker every time Mia saw him.

Mia had been daydreaming – but now the words of a plump, elderly contessa crawled in between her dreams. 'Why don't they send her away? I declare, it makes my skin crawl to look at her. Her Grace is far too forgiving.' The voice hissed in her ears, dry and snake-like, and Mia burned inside. That contessa had smiled sweetly at Mia for years and fed her sugared almonds. Had everyone been lying to her, always?

She ducked her head, staring down at her pretty embroidered slippers, biting her lip till it bled, so she wouldn't let them see her cry. When the audience ended, she hurried back to her rooms and dismissed her maids. She cut the strings of her tight bodice herself, with a paperknife, tearing away the stiff shell of the dress so she could breathe again. She was gasping for air, sucking in great sobbing gulps of it as she listened to the voices over and over in her head. Her mouth was filled with the cloying sweetness of those almonds.

Then Mia sensed something shift and open inside her. She could almost hear the cracking of the shell, feel the magic seeping out. For a glorious moment, she let it spill through her. Was this what it felt like to be a magician? To be like Olivia and Signor Jac, and all those other mages of the court?

Then she whirled round, kicking away the spoiled dress and clutching her arms across her chest in a sudden burst of fear and horror. She would not! She couldn't! She would *never* be like Olivia and the others – and not like her mother, either. Everyone was waiting, and watching for her magic – her treachery. Let them watch.

Mia crouched down by the side of her bed again, kneeling on the floor. She curled up like a tight, dry seed, clenching her fists, her teeth. Even her eyes were screwed tight shut.

Go away. Go back. Never, never, never, never—

She broke off, gasping, shivering all over in a strange fit, like the ague that had come drifting in off the sticky summer waters the year before, when half the court had taken to their beds. She felt sick, and shuddered – but the unfurling, growing magic inside her was gone.

Mia lay on the floor in her bedchamber, hidden by the great carved bed, in case someone should peer around the door looking for her. A few thin bars of afternoon sunlight crept around the cracks in the shutters and glowed sharp and golden on the embroidered rug by the side of the bed. Mia watched them move, so slowly, her eyes unfocused and still a little swollen from tears. She felt so ill, so weak, that she couldn't move from her curled shape on the floor.

When her maids discovered her at last, they were convinced that it was indeed some fever that had gripped her. She was put to bed, fussed over and dosed…and left to dream of mergirls, and a frantic, hopeless game of chase.

CHAPTER TWO

MIA STOOD AT THE DOOR of the water chamber, behind the curtains. There was a bald patch on the cloth, she realised, with a tiny smile. She had hidden here so many times, clutching at the velvet with angry fingers, that the pile was almost worn away.

The room was empty – she had woken early from her dream and none of the rest of the court was about, only the servants. She had strolled proudly past several curious maids on her way through the palace.

She'd expected that one or two of the water horses would be here sleeping still, but they must have woken already. There was no reason why she shouldn't go in – even if there had been others there. She was the duchess's cousin. In theory, she was Olivia's heir, as well. She could go anywhere in the palace, even the Council Room, should she wish to. She didn't wish to, of course, as most of the council thought that she should have been exiled with her mother, and that she ought to be kept under close guard at least, for everyone else's safety.

She had woken from the dream desperate and angry. Why did she keep seeing these things? She hated the water, she *had* to – that was part of her now. She had to be everything that her cousin was not. But her dreams betrayed her, and now she wanted to be by the sea. She needed more than staring down at the canal from her window. Something inside her was dragging her there – and this time she couldn't banish the darting figures from her mind. She *needed* the water, and the water chamber was the only place she could go, for a nobly-born girl couldn't wander along the canals by herself, although Olivia had always seemed to manage it, from the stories everyone told. But Mia had no desire to go climbing out of windows – she didn't have the magic to make herself float, or a water horse to catch her.

Glancing behind her, she hurried down the steps into the great room. The water was low, and so only the central channel that led out into the lagoon was full, and the tethered platforms lay still on the marble floor. Mia hurried along the side of the channel and out onto the seaward part of the chamber, the horseshoe-shaped floating pavilion where her cousin consulted with the creatures of the sea.

It was an odd room, built of wood, and only attached to the main part of the palace by long chains, so that it could rise and fall with the tides. Its two halves curved out facing each other, leaving an open channel between for the water horses to swim to the inner chamber. The pavilion had a strange, rather makeshift look, as it was furnished to look grand, but at the same time to be waterproof. There were a great many oilskin cushions, and most of the furniture was wooden and fantastically carved. The rest of the palace was much more heavy and dark, with great falls of curtains and thick tapestries. The pavilion was airy and cold, the breeze blowing in off the lagoon with a tang of salt and fish.

Mia arranged the long skirts of her embroidered dressing robe carefully, and sat down at the very edge. Then she sighed, and lay face down on the gilded boards instead. No one was here, so she didn't have to be dignified. It made her feel like a carefree child again, when she had run out here away from her nursemaids, eager to be grown up. She used to lie here and watch the water then, dipping her hands and splashing. Now she realised that the water horses had been swimming next to her, watching her more carefully and lovingly than the nursemaids ever did. She missed them so.

Mia shook away the sudden longing, and trailed her hand in the greenish water. She shivered – not from the water's chill, but from the way it reminded her of the dream. That sudden shock of silky cold. Were they really down there? The *mermaids*? Surely they were just a fairy tale, the kind of story that much smaller children loved. That was it. It was just a remembered story, something told to a smaller, happier child, a long time ago.

It seemed so real, though. She knew the girls in the water – she watched them almost every night, she swam with them. She couldn't have imagined them all out of nothing…

It's just because you're lonely, she told herself firmly. *You've made yourself a whole lot of friends that no one else can see.*

But the horses were real, so why not the girls in the water too? And other things – she was sure she had seen other creatures in her dreams, just not so clearly. As though they were further away. She seemed to remember a great, dark eye, so huge that it ought to have been terrifying, but it wasn't. If she was going to believe in the mermaids, then the eye's owner was there too – a gentle, curious watcher in the water.

But she didn't truly believe in mermaids. It was a *dream*. That was all. She was dreaming it more and more now because she was worried.

It didn't mean anything.

The peace of the water spread through her, floating away the panicked, hurried gossiping. Mia felt as though it had never stopped, this last few weeks, this fear of war coming to Venice. *Were they coming? Would they invade? What would it mean for the great families, for the city, for the duchess?* The courtiers twittered and whispered like a flock of panicked little birds and Mia had longed to swoop out into the middle of the audience chamber and swirl them away. She would be one of those huge yellow-eyed seagulls and scatter the lot of them.

She laughed to herself, and dabbled the tips of her fingers in the water, stirring it up into little bouncing ripples. All the whispers – and the whisperers – would be swept away as the gull soared by. It was so hard to sit and smile and wave her fan, and wonder if there was any truth in it at all. Even though Mia knew that the court was obsessed with rumours – stupid, baseless whisperings, like that of her own treachery, or about Olivia dyeing her hair by magic – it was hard not to listen, when people kept on and on saying the same thing. Yesterday, before she went on to discussing Mia's own deceitful nature, the contessa had been making dire predictions of war.

'The Talish ambassador has been sending messengers back and forth for weeks,' she fluted triumphantly. 'Weeks and weeks, you know. Of course, the Emperor is quite decided. If Duchess Olivia won't marry his son, they'll invade. It's quite settled.'

How on earth does she know? Mia thought to herself, sitting quietly on the steps next to her cousin's throne. Olivia was discussing something with her councillors, and not listening to the contessa's thin, quavery voice.

'Of course, my dear son Benedict knows everything that's going on.' The contessa nodded grandly.

'He has the ear of the duchess, you see. He is one of her most trusted advisors.'

Actually, she thinks he's an idiot. Mia suppressed a smirk. She might not be on speaking terms with her cousin, but she only had to look at the fixed smile on Olivia's face when the count started paying her flowery compliments to know that she couldn't stand the fool.

The two young ladies-in-waiting who were sitting with the contessa nodded, wide-eyed. 'Whatever will happen to us all?' the dark-haired one whispered. 'Duchess Olivia must marry him, surely? She couldn't be so selfish not to!'

'Not with all those ships just outside the lagoon, waiting to pounce…' The plump little lady-in-waiting shuddered. 'We'll be overrun. I'm quite certain they'll fire the city – my sister says those ships are simply laden with casks of oil and spirits. They'll even set fire to the canals. Her maid told her so, she had it from one of the gondoliers, and he'd been out to look at the ships, so of course he must know.'

The ships…

Mia looked out across the lagoon, half shutting her eyes and squinting to see if she could see them. There was a faint smudge on the far horizon, but she couldn't decide if it was just a cloud. Everyone in the palace seemed certain that the ships were there, but Mia wasn't sure – it could just be panicky gossip.

The Talish ambassador was most definitely real. He had been passing on the Emperor's polite threats for over a year, and now the threats were becoming less polite by the day. The Talish had been eyeing up Venice for centuries. The Emperor envied the city's trade network almost as much as he wanted the secrets of the great shipbuilders in the Arsenale. The water magic had lingered in the shipbuilding workshops as a set of rhymes and knacks and secret signs, even as it had dwindled away throughout the rest of the city. The shipbuilders never called it magic – it was just those little tricks they did, to make their beauties sail sleeker, trimmer, faster. Venetian ships were the glory of the city.

Mia could see several of them now, moored out in the lagoon, ready, their beaked sterns turned hawkishly towards that dark line on the horizon. They looked ready. But they weren't enough, or so everyone was whispering. The Talish Empire was so very big, and so very rich. There were ships in their hundreds, lurking out there beyond the lagoon. Even the magically swift Venetian galleys and frigates could be surrounded.

The ambassador had suggested a series of trade treaties that the council had called insulting. Why should Venice give up most of the profits of her spice trade with the East? Why should their great ships fight the Emperor's wars for him? They had put him off, again and again, ducking around the promises the ambassador argued for. But the Emperor had sent an ultimatum, demanding an alliance – which really meant that Venice would become part of the Empire in all but name.

Who knew what the Talish would do, to tear out the city's secrets? The power of the water horses to control the tides and the floods – what could the Empire do with that? Panicked rumours ran round the city, a new one every day. The duchess would be imprisoned. The canals were to be filled in. The city would be mined for its magic, and then abandoned. Ever more frightening stories were swapped over the sides of gondolas, passed on in shops, whispered from window to window.

Mia had been present in the audience chamber two weeks before, when the ambassador had finally revealed his hand. He had made a long speech in his low, purring voice, praising Venice and her ships, and the magic that seemed to whisper in the air and water of the city. So beautiful, so strong – just like the duchess. It seemed to go on for hours, that speech, full of honeyed flattery. And then, the ambassador had at last come to the point. Mia had seen the sudden glitter in his narrow black eyes. This was the real meat of it.

To seal the treaty, the Emperor wanted a wedding, between the little duchess and his son, the young

Prince Leo. The ambassador waved one white hand, and a page boy ran up with the prince's portrait, in a heavy, jewelled frame. He knelt to offer it to the duchess, and then another boy darted forwards with a pair of fine hounds, with pale, spotted coats and yellowish eyes.

The boy had handed their leashes to Mia, and she stood there with the fine red leather of the leashes wrapped around her fingers, wondering what to do with the creatures as they snuffled and scratched. Then both of them had raised their heads at once, and their yellow eyes glinted as they yanked their leashes from Mia's hand. They had seen the strange brown cat that belonged to Olivia's maid. Coco had been stretched out beneath the throne, but now he stalked out onto the steps and stared at them, and spat. Then he seemed to be suddenly a great deal larger than he'd been before, with a heavy ruff of fur around his neck. The hounds ran back to the page who'd brought them, wild-eyed and whimpering.

The ambassador eyed Mia coldly, and then forced

a smile onto his face and began to make profuse apologies, his white hands fluttering in the air as he described how desolated he was to have disturbed the peace of the dear duchess's court with the ill-bred hounds. He would have them drowned at once.

Olivia had gasped at that, and shaken her head, and the ambassador smiled. 'So soft-hearted, Your Grace,' he murmured. 'I shall tell Prince Leo of your sweet nature, your sympathetic heart. He will be delighted.'

Olivia's mouth was set in a line, so that she didn't look sweet-natured at all. But she managed to nod, and murmur something diplomatic about consulting with her advisors before undertaking anything so important as a marriage.

The dogs were taken away by one of the councillors, who had a fine house on one of the islands, with space for a pair of hounds to run wild, but he'd told Mia that they were not much use as hunting dogs now. Even a squirrel could make them turn tail and run for home.

The portrait and the hounds were supposed to be love gifts, but the ships came with them, lurking just out of sight. Waiting. Already, several of the great families had left, finding sudden reasons to travel for business, or visit relatives in one of the other great cities, one that hadn't yet caught the Emperor's attention. Everyone else looked to the duchess and the council, and waited to be saved.

'Couldn't you tell them to go away?' Mia whispered to the water. Then she grimaced, laughing at herself, talking to her dream-creatures, like a silly baby. But with her fingers swirling in the water, the dreams felt so clear and real. She could almost hear the mermaids talking back.

Then she rolled over with a gasp, snatching her hands out of the water. The voices were from behind her, on the steps into the water chambers.

'They really are here, then?'

'Signor Lucian is quite sure? I mean, a horse...? How can he be sure what he's seeing?'

'A water horse, remember, he knows more about

the lagoon than any man alive.'

Mia looked down at herself, automatically smoothing and straightening her skirts as she scrambled to her feet. But it was no good. She was wearing a dressing robe – made from beautiful brocade with a knotted silk braid on the sleeves and round the hem, but still a dressing robe, over her nightgown. And the sleeves were wet. She hadn't even brushed her hair.

She glanced around quickly and then scurried behind a wooden chest, a great dark thing that was used to store cushions and rugs away from the damp night air. It was still early. Hopefully, whoever was coming wouldn't be here for long – not long enough to want to pull out a rug, anyway.

She crouched behind the chest, scarlet-cheeked, hoping that it was only the servants, come to sweep and freshen the rooms and gossiping while they were at it. Probably she should have stood her ground and told them she couldn't sleep, that she'd come for the cooler air. But now she was hiding, and they'd find her, and it would be all around the palace in a day. The duchess's strange, treacherous little cousin hiding behind the furniture.

Then a rippling, splashing sound made her glance sideways, and the chamber rocked suddenly as a great white creature leapt out of the sea, his mane and tail spilling water over the fretted floor. It drained away at once, leaving only a glistening dampness on the gilding, and the water horse shook his mane and snorted, casting himself down at the very edge of the chamber. One of his forelegs trailed into the water and he glanced behind him impatiently, watching for the others who were walking in from the palace.

'How many are there, Lucian?' someone asked, someone whose light, pattering footsteps hurried out into the pavilion.

Mia sighed. Of course. It was her cousin, and from the sound of the deeper, worried voices following after her, Olivia was accompanied by half the council – the half that hadn't run away. She peered cautiously around the edge of the chest, trying to see which of the councillors were there.

'Upwards of four hundred,' the horse rumbled reluctantly. 'A mixture of oared galleons, and those big things. Whatever they're called, the ones with the silly name.'

'Ships of the line,' Mia's cousin sighed. 'Warships. You're sure.'

'Yes, those. Dirty great wooden crates. They smell. They stir up the waters. Things will rise.' He let out an angry snort.

'I know...'

Her cousin seemed to understand at once what the huge horse meant by *things*, and Mia's heart jumped a little inside her, after a night spent deep underwater, surrounded by laughing mergirls. Was the water horse talking about the creatures she had seen in her dreams? Were they really there? If only she could ask!

'Your Grace...' gasped one of the lords of the council. Mia could see that they had caught Olivia up, and were standing around their duchess, draped in heavy cloaks, short of breath. 'Your Grace, does

Signor Lucian have any news? Are they preparing to attack?'

'How would I know?' growled the horse. 'There are sailors scurrying all over them like ants, that's all I can see.'

'Four hundred ships, Lord Marco.' Mia heard the catch in her cousin's voice, and flinched. 'Perhaps I should marry him, and send those ships away from our city.'

'Nonsense, Your Grace!' another of the men put in angrily. 'You can't give in to them.'

'Then what do we do?' Mia heard her cousin's hasty footsteps as she rounded on the council. 'You heard Lucian – four hundred ships! We can't fight that many. Frankly, I'm surprised they haven't attacked us already. Must I let our entire navy be killed or captured, and *then* marry the prince? Wouldn't it be better to give in gracefully?'

'They haven't attacked because they suspect you have more magic than you're letting on,' Lucian murmured.

'Really?' Olivia's voice lifted in surprise.

'I imagine that's true, Your Grace,' Lord Marco agreed, trudging over to stand by the water's edge. From the little she could see, Mia decided he must be staring out at the ships. 'They don't know what you can unleash on them, if they attack. Your powers are very great – and they've been talked over endlessly, these last few years. The Talish ambassador saw the way you drew back the floods, remember. And he was on the ship when you broke Lady Sofia's spells. He's seen your magic, Your Grace, and he's reported back to his master. They've been discussed endlessly, in every court. The Emperor has come to believe that you're a danger. And now that our merchants have taken so much of the spice trade away from their Talish counterparts, he's been persuaded to do something about it. If we hinted to the Emperor that you could create a great water dragon who would blow his fleet back to their home port in pieces, he'd probably believe us.'

'Would that help?' Lucian enquired.

There was a moment's shocked silence, and then Lord Marco carried on, his voice a little shaken. 'Well, yes, I suppose so… Your Grace, I suggested a dragon made of water as a – as a silly example. *Could* you do that?'

Mia edged round the chest a little, listening curiously. Could she?

'If I had all the horses, and Signor Jac and his companions, and we exhausted ourselves, perhaps,' Olivia agreed. 'But we would have infuriated the Emperor, and drained our magic. What good would it do?'

'You could destroy their fleet?' Lord Marco demanded sharply.

'No!' Mia shrank back as her cousin's voice rose. 'No… I couldn't…'

'Your Grace, we cannot afford to be soft-hearted.'

'How many men would be aboard those four hundred ships, Lord Marco?'

Silence again, and then a gusty sigh. 'I don't know, Your Grace. Thousands. Tens of thousands.'

'It's very easy to be the hard-hearted one, Lord Marco, when it isn't you that kills them all.'

'Them or us,' someone else muttered.

'Perhaps,' Olivia murmured. 'But we don't know for sure that we could destroy their fleet, my lords. What if they have their own magicians aboard? We could let loose a storm of magic that would kill us all.'

'Is *she* there?'

Mia flinched. She recognised that voice, and now the plain dark clothes of the man who came to stand beside her cousin. She hadn't realised that Signor Jac was in the room. The duchess's advisor frightened her. He had magic that was almost as powerful as Olivia's own, but his magic spilled out of him in strange lights and shimmers, hardly under control at all. He strode through the palace crowds with a wildness in his dark eyes that made Mia think of a creature caged.

'I don't know,' Olivia whispered.

'You can't tell?' He spoke to her so sharply that Mia felt shocked despite herself. He shouldn't talk to her cousin like that... Mia scowled, and shook her head a little. *She* didn't care how anyone spoke to Olivia.

'No.'

There was a thud of hooves, and a soft snorting, and the platform shook a little as the water horse went to comfort Olivia.

'She is, of course she is,' Signor Jac muttered. 'It was a mistake to send her into exile. She has whipped the Emperor up into this invasion frenzy. It's her revenge. This is how she'll put that idiot son of hers on the throne. Ha! So she thinks, anyway.'

'But the Emperor wants his own son to marry Her Grace. And the people would never accept Lord Zuan, not as a puppet for the Talish,' Lord Marco argued.

'I shouldn't think Zuan cares much about the people's opinion,' Olivia sighed. 'Yes, Jac, I suspect that my aunt is there. Lady Sofia is known to have been at the Talish court, and a great favourite of the Emperor. Who knows what she's planning? I can't see how she could make Zuan the duke now, but she always did plan far ahead.'

Mia stuffed her hand into her mouth to stop herself from squeaking. They were talking about Olivia's aunt! *Her mother!* Her mother was coming back, at last. She sat curled behind the chest, trembling, convinced that her heart was thumping so loudly it must give her away any moment. She had never thought that this would happen.

Out in the chamber, her cousin and the council were murmuring worriedly together. One of the lords was suggesting a visit to the shipyards, to see if the new warships in dry dock could be hurried along – to even the numbers a little. Mia hardly heard them. All she cared about was that they were going.

She would be alone again, to think – to plan.

CHAPTER THREE

A S THE HEAVY FOOTSTEPS died away, Mia walked out from behind the chest, stumbling a little. If she hadn't had that dream – if she hadn't given in and let herself go down to the water – she might never have known.

Her mother! She could be there, just out at the horizon, hardly any distance at all. Her mother had come to take her back. Her mother and Zuan, they would be so pleased to see her!

Something twisted inside and Mia shook her head

angrily, brushing the thought away. They couldn't have sent letters to her, of course they couldn't. A letter from Lady Sofia would have been read by the palace guard and her cousin, and then destroyed. But couldn't her mother have sent some sort of a message? If she had been in Talis all this time? Wouldn't there have been something she could do? A message through the ambassador, perhaps. Just so that Mia knew they were still alive!

The ambassador... Mia stopped at the water's edge, gripping the side of the wooden wall, where the pavilion opened out onto the sea. If he had come to her with a secret message from her mother, she would probably have run away. He was horrible – thin and spidery-limbed, and so unctuously polite. He looked at Mia as though he knew every hateful thought she had about her cousin. He made her feel as though she really was a traitor.

And so I would be, she thought suddenly. *If I see my mother and brother again, it will be because Venice is lost. The Talish will have won, and taken the city. I don't want that...do I?*

Mia looked at the milky-green water, slapping gently against the side of the pavilion, her eyes filling with tears. She hated her cousin so deeply for exiling her family. She had refused her magic because she felt Olivia had betrayed her, and tried to crush the deep love she had for the creatures of the water. She had spent nearly three years pretending she couldn't see the magic in the water. She had pretended so well that she was almost convinced. It was only that she couldn't stop herself from dreaming of the creatures in the sea. But she was still tied to the city – how could she choose between her family and Venice?

'My mother would come back here to live,' she whispered to the water. 'I'd still be here. Nothing would change.' But she knew it wasn't true. Her cousin belonged to Venice. Olivia was part of the city, and the city's magic ran in her blood. Venice would never be the same without her. Even if Olivia married Prince Leo, and she was still the duchess in name, Venice would be just another part of the Empire.

And the magic... It was the one rumour that rang true, she thought. *If Venice became part of the Empire, her secrets would belong to the Empire too. What would they do to the horses?* She shivered, thinking about it, imagining them led away in chains, hauled on board ships, or perhaps dragged behind, all the way to Talis. And there they would be shut away in great, stinking tanks. They would test them with ugly spells, until their deep, secret magic was known, and stored away in books.

'I can't...' Mia whispered miserably. 'I don't know what to do.'

She could go to the ambassador now – part of her wanted to, so much. She could go creeping through the palace to his quarters, and she could tell him what her cousin had said. That she would never attack the fleet, because she couldn't bear to kill all those men. If the Talish knew that, they would probably invade at once. She could demand to be taken to her mother, in exchange for her information. She would say that there was more she could tell, but only to Lady Sofia. She could do it…

Mia gasped, her vision filling with glittering threads. It was like her dream again, the embroidery on her mother's dress unravelling and spiralling around her. Did that mean that her mother was close? Just out there across the water? Mia took another step towards the edge, reaching out. Her mother's magic was so strong, everyone said so. Couldn't she hear her daughter calling? Surely she knew Mia was there, and wishing for her. She imagined her mother on board one of the great ships, leaping to her feet in a gilded stateroom and rushing up onto the deck.

'Fetch me,' she begged, as the threads swirled in the air and she staggered closer to the edge. 'Can't you just fetch me? Call me over with a spell. I'd come, I would…' She reached out across the water, trying to haul the threads in, to draw her mother to her. She could feel the bonds tightening – they were there! They wanted her! Someone wanted her…

The long skirt of her dressing robe trailed in the water as she leant out, and a few sparkling drops flicked cold across the scrap of bare skin that showed above the embroidered satin of her slippers.

All at once the golden threads around her heart slackened, and thinned to almost nothing. For a moment, Mia felt empty, unloved again. Then the delicious coolness of the water, seeping slowly over her skin, brought her back to her dream. She closed her eyes for a moment, shutting out the glittering of the sun on the water and sinking down into the green depths of the lagoon. Jewelled tails vanished around the ribbons of weed, and dark eyes peered out at her. Pale fingers beckoned, and someone laughed in a stream of bubbles.

She couldn't leave.

The magic of the city ran in her blood too, however much she'd begged it not to be there. Her mother and her brother had betrayed the city and broken away, but Mia couldn't bring herself to do the same.

'What do I do?' She leant over, peering at her own

shaky reflection in the water. She was the only person she could talk to, after all. A greenish version of herself stared back, pale-skinned, with light hair like tarnished metal, but the girl in the water didn't have anything to say.

'I can't stay here, and I can't leave,' she whispered, and the pale girl gazed back at her. 'The older I get, the more frightened of me everyone will be. I hate it – even my ladies-in-waiting are scared to be in a room with me, in case I'm secretly planning to enchant them all.' She sniffed, then laughed. 'I wish I could. If I had any magic in me, I'd enchant them into saying something interesting occasionally. I don't think I can live like this much longer.'

A faint shadow stirred under the water, brushing over her face, and just for a moment Mia saw a tail flick past, scales shimmering. She smiled to herself – sunlight on the water, a strand of weed swaying in the current. That was all. Wasn't it?

'Lucian and Olivia said that there *were* other things down there,' she murmured softly. She swallowed, her mouth suddenly dry. 'Are you there? Are there other creatures, as well as the horses? Tell me, please!'

There was nothing. The faint echo of her question died away into the sound of the water. The sea was still and cold and empty, and Mia pressed her hands against her eyes, forcing back her tears. Of course there was nothing.

Her head ached, from fear and excitement and trying not to cry, and the quiet emptiness of the water looked welcoming, even if it had been only a dream and there were no mermaids. What would happen if she stepped in? Would anyone miss her? How long would it take them to know that she was gone? If Mia gave herself to the water, she would never have to worry. She would never have to *decide*.

Mia stared down at herself and watched as a tear splashed into the sea. Just one tear, sending a shimmer across her reflection. There didn't seem much point in crying.

When the tiny ripple smoothed away, the face was different – wider across the cheekbones, the eyes suddenly huge and dark. Mia blinked, thinking that more tears were blurring her sight, but when she looked again, the features were even clearer, and she could see a swirl of dark reddish hair floating around the face.

It wasn't her reflection. There was another girl gazing at her out of the water, frowning at Mia, biting her lip anxiously as she broke the surface.

They stared at each other for a moment, and then Mia sat down hard, folding up onto the floor. Her legs were shaking – she'd hardly slept and she hadn't eaten, so maybe this was just another strange waking dream?

But the girl didn't look like a dream – and in her dreams, she had only seen the mermaids in the water, flickering around her, disappearing in and out of the weeds. She had never seen one face to face, like this.

The girl rested her arms on the wooden floor of the pavilion, and looked up at Mia. Her skin was as pale as Mia's own, and flecked with water drops. Her hair coiled dripping over her shoulders, thick and red like seaweed, the kind that washed up on the sandy beaches of the islands. Waterweed was bound around her chest, but to a child raised in the court and taught to wear layers upon layers of indulgent fabrics, her arms and shoulders were shockingly bare. Mia could see the darkly glinting bulk of her tail as a shadow in the water.

'I dreamed you,' Mia whispered. 'I've seen you before, I think.'

The girl nodded. 'You swam with us,' she said, her voice low and husky.

'But – I can't have, really.' Mia frowned at her. 'I can't swim. I've never even been in the water, except riding on one of the water horses.'

The girl shrugged expressively, and the weed-like mass of her hair rippled. 'You were there. I remember. Perhaps you travel in your dreams. It can be done.'

'I know your voice too,' Mia said slowly. 'I've heard you singing.' She looked down at her arms, covered by the thick silk brocade of her robe, and slid back one sleeve, pinching herself hard, hard enough to leave a whiter dent in her pale indoor skin. The whiteness coloured over again, a shade darker than before, and the girl in the water was still there. 'Not a dream,' Mia whispered. 'Real.' And then she added, almost angrily, 'Why did you come now? Why didn't you ever show me that you were real before? I thought I was being stupid, that I'd made you up.'

The mermaid shrugged again. 'You never called before,' she reminded Mia, but her eyes slid sideways, as though that wasn't the whole of the truth. 'You were just there, sometimes, swimming with us. We never knew when you would come, and you were never there for long. A dream-child, sometimes there and sometimes not. You were a little girl in a white dress, and you never spoke, to tell us who you were. You just smiled at us, out of the waterweeds, and watched. Sometimes you'd follow us out into the open water, but not often. Mostly you just watched.'

'And listened,' Mia said, remembering. It felt as though the dreams were settling in her mind, like sand in water. They were clearing. 'You sang to each other, but I didn't understand the words. It wasn't the way you're speaking now. I *felt* you singing.' She smiled, thinking of the tides, the relentless pull of the water, and its steady power. All these things she knew, without knowing. 'You sang to me about the sea,' she murmured. 'But I didn't remember that it was real when I woke up. I thought it was only dreaming. I thought I was strange. I *knew* I was different. Everyone said.'

'You are strange,' the mermaid agreed. 'An odd little land girl. We'd never seen one up so close. You frightened us. If you hadn't been so small, we might have chased you away. But all you did was smile and watch, and after a while it didn't seem so wrong for you to be there.'

Mia nodded. 'I still can't understand how I was there enough for you to see me,' she murmured. 'How can I have been dreaming all of this? It makes no sense. In all those dreams, I was in the water? But I never came back wet.' She laughed to herself. There was a mermaid in front of her. Talking to her.

The strange dreams she'd had for years were true – she could think about *how* later on. 'I suppose it's magic,' she said slowly. 'Maybe I do have some strange sort of magic in me after all. You really came because I called you?'

The girl nodded, and rested her chin on her arms. She still looked worried. 'You were with us again last night, and then you disappeared so suddenly. You were there, and then you'd simply gone, and your face was frightened, just for that moment. I tried to find you – I didn't understand how you could disappear, and I thought you must just be hiding somewhere. Then it seemed as though I knew where you were. I don't understand how it happened, perhaps it was because you had your hands in the water? So I came to see. You called, and I was there in the water, below you. I was watching, and I wanted to answer you. I wanted to see what you were like, when you were back on the land. But I couldn't – we don't ever show ourselves to humans. I had to watch, that was all.'

'But you did – you *are* showing yourself to me.'

The mermaid looked behind her at the water. 'I know. I shouldn't be, but I recognised you – you are the same child we've seen in the sea. I *know* you, even though we've never spoken. I've known you for years. Then I saw you staring into the water, and there was a look in your eyes I'd seen before, on other poor sad creatures. You were going to step in. And all at once I could see that you weren't the same child, after all. If you took that step, you wouldn't swim with us, you couldn't. And you knew it.'

'I wasn't going to,' Mia whispered, closing her eyes.

'You were.'

'I thought about it for a moment, that's all. Because I couldn't see what else to do.' She was glad her eyes were closed, and she didn't have to see the other girl's face. She was sure the mermaid was disgusted with her. 'It seemed as though it might be easier. The water looked – gentle.'

'It isn't. Not for you, not ever.'

'You don't know that!' Mia opened her eyes and

glared at the mermaid. How could this water creature know what her life in the palace was like? 'How do you know what's happening to me? You don't know anything!'

The mermaid flicked her mass of reddish hair and sniffed, as though she wasn't impressed by Mia's little tantrum. 'Tell me, then.' She glanced behind her at the water again, and then up at the stone bulk of the palace. 'But not here. Come on.'

'Come on where?' Mia demanded suspiciously.

The mermaid smiled at her, her dark eyes glinting. 'Where else? Into the water.'

CHAPTER FOUR

MIA WAS SO ANGRY SHE actually stamped her foot. What was it about the mermaid that made her so cross? 'I can't! You just said it yourself – I'll drown.'

The mermaid sighed, and rolled her eyes. 'I know that, silly land girl. We'll stay on the surface but I'll take you somewhere we can talk. I can't stay here – someone will see me. Either one of your people, or one of mine.'

'No one else knows you're here…' Mia said slowly.

'Haven't I explained? I'm not allowed to be talking to you! Your people are too dangerous to mine.' The mermaid slapped the wooden floor of the pavilion impatiently. 'We never speak to you, not ever. If one of my sisters did this, I would be angry, don't you see? I would be the one demanding that she be walled up in one of the dead dark places under the sea. I would want her where she couldn't put the rest of us in danger any more. And I would be right. But I'm doing this anyway! Now, will you come or not?'

Mia looked at the water, the hugeness of it, and licked her suddenly dry lips. She wasn't sure she actually wanted to do this, but she was going to. 'Yes.'

The mermaid backed away from the pavilion a little, holding out her hands to Mia. 'Come on, then.'

Mia set her mouth in a hard line – she had never thought much about what the mermaids would be like to talk to. She had tried so hard to banish those dreams. But she had always assumed they would be *nicer*. This sharp-tongued, rather grumpy mermaid wasn't what she had expected at all.

Still, if the mergirl had been nicer, she would probably have dithered on the edge, Mia realised. She would have protested that she couldn't, that she was frightened, that she didn't know how to swim. Faced with a contemptuous mermaid, she slipped off the dressing robe and her slippers and stuffed them at the back of the chest with the blankets. Then she sat down on the edge of the floor, and put her feet in the water. She didn't even close her eyes. She stared grimly back at the mermaid, who looked as though she was trying not to smirk, and edged further in. The water slapped cold against her, and her nightgown stuck wetly to her legs.

Mia tried not to shiver. Even though she was a traitor's daughter, she was still a member of the ruling family of the city. Her washing water came steaming hot, poured into an elegant bowl by her maid, who also had an armful of fresh linen towels. When Mia wanted a bath, the fire would be lit in the little room next to her bedroom, and buckets and buckets of hot water sent up from the kitchens. The maids would pour the water into the copper bath, which stood on smart clawed feet, and then scent the water with precious spiced oils. Mia climbed into the bath up a little flight of gilded steps. Cold, dirty, greenish seawater was a shock – but she wasn't going to let the mergirl see that. Mia reached out for her hands, and let the girl pull her that last step into the water, her nightgown billowing around her like a huge white flower.

'You did it,' the mermaid said, sounding impressed despite herself. 'I thought you'd run back to your palace.'

'It's so cold,' Mia stuttered, as a great shiver ran through her, slamming her teeth together with an uncontrollable rattle. The water lapped around her face and she gasped, fighting to keep her mouth and nose out of it. There was a strange feeling in the bones at the back of her neck and around her ears, a whispery, watery feeling, as though the water had seeped inside her.

'Because it's deep,' the mergirl murmured in her

ear, wrapping her arms around Mia, so that they swam together like dancers promenading at a ball.

Mia could feel the mermaid's tail, scaled and muscular, as it beat their way through the water. The strength of it daunted her a little – the mermaids had always seemed so delicate in her dreams. It felt so strange – not just to be held against a tail, but to be held at all. Mia no longer let Olivia embrace her – she suffered her cousin's polite ritual kisses, but that was all. She never sat curled up on a sofa, leaning against her ladies-in-waiting, or strolled arm in arm with anyone along the piazza.

Even in the deep cold of the water, however, the mergirl's arms around her were warm. Mia twisted her neck round, peering over her shoulder, and the mermaid turned with her, stretching out on her back and holding Mia at arm's length so that she could see. Her tail coiled and flickered in the water, and Mia longed to stroke it. It glimmered with the same oiled radiance as the fish she had seen lying on slabs of ice when she'd gone sneaking into the palace kitchens.

But even through the water it was a rich golden amber colour, each scale red-edged. She had seen nothing like those gleaming scales on a fish, even a fish that was to be served to a duchess.

'Now do you believe?' the mermaid whispered in her ear, and she flashed sharp white teeth in a grin.

'Yes...' Mia breathed, watching the red and gold tail fin swish lazily from side to side.

'Good. Now we need to swim – it's too busy here, boats everywhere. I have a little magic to hide us with, but not enough.'

'You can do magic too, then?' Mia said breathlessly, as the mermaid hauled her through the water, the tail now beating rapidly from front to back. The way it coiled reminded Mia of an eel, and she shuddered a little. Her cousin's court ate great banquets of fish, and Mia had seen eels in tanks of seawater in the kitchens, waiting to be served up fresh as a delicacy. They writhed around each other like snakes, with sharp-nosed, toothy faces.

Until then, she hadn't thought about what else

might be swimming around them. Lobsters perhaps, all claws and feelers, or jellyfish? Something touched her foot and Mia flinched – it was probably just a strand of waterweed, but she couldn't stop thinking of purple and red stinging tentacles. She'd seen them at a distance, when she was dreaming, and they'd looked so beautiful, but now she was in the water for real, not as a dream visitor. What if the mermaid dragged her through those poisoned trails without knowing? Mermaids probably didn't get stung.

There could be sharks, even. Years before, a fisherman had shown her the carcass of a shark that had tangled itself in his nets. He had been trying to impress the lady-in-waiting who had been walking with Mia along the waterfront, but the shark had terrified the older girl. She had tried to drag Mia away, squeaking about its huge teeth and tiny, evil eyes, but Mia had felt sorry for the great creature. Its eyes had been like dull stones, and its skin was cracking in the heat. It seemed so unfair – the fisherman hadn't even been trying to catch it, and now he was famous, with people coming from all over the city to see the fearsome beast.

She didn't want to remember the shark's smooth bulk now, the shape made to cut through the water – and those teeth… She pressed closer against the mergirl and curled her toes.

'Can't you at least kick?' the mermaid snapped, panting a little. 'You're so heavy. Do something with your feet. Like you did under the water – you could swim then.'

'That wasn't me,' Mia tried to explain. 'Not really me. Or at any rate, I wasn't awake enough to know about it.' But she tried, wafting her feet through the water, surprised by how hard it was to press against – not like a liquid at all.

'Like that,' the mermaid coughed out. 'Not much further now.'

She darted behind a tiny fishing boat, moored at anchor, with a boy curled up asleep on the stern. There were ropes dangling over the side, and Mia guessed he must have lobster pots or fish traps set.

'Here.'

A few metres further on from the boat, the water changed colour to a milky jade-green, and it grew suddenly warmer. Mia only realised then how cold she had been as her stiff fingers began to ache. The mermaid dropped her in the soupy, shallow water and crawled exhaustedly onto a patch of sand, settling back on her elbows, with her glorious tail spreading into the water. Mia clambered out after her, sitting with her arms huddled around her knees. The sand was wet and muddy brown, but so deliciously, blissfully warm. She shivered, thinking of the journey back.

'Is this Sant'Erasmo?' she murmured, squinting, and trying to see landmarks. 'The sandbar off the island?'

The mermaid shrugged. 'Perhaps. We have our own names. We don't come this far in very often. Just sometimes, to lie on the sand and feel the sun on our hair.'

Mia turned back to look at her – the red hair was

spreading down over her shoulders now and trailing on the sand. It was beautiful in the sun, all shades of red and orange and purple, with even an odd golden-green strand here and there. She could just imagine the whole patch of sand covered in fishtailed girls, their hair coiled around them, gossiping and preening in the sun.

'You all come here?' she murmured, looking around. 'So close to the city?'

'Only sometimes, like I said. It takes effort, hiding ourselves this close in. It's easy to forget, and then someone hears a phrase or two of one of our songs…' She slapped her tail fin against the water, sending up a shower of sunlit spray.

'What happens? They tell?'

The mergirl shook her head. 'Our songs aren't meant for you people to hear. They're too powerful. Too dangerous for you.' She frowned thoughtfully at Mia. 'You might be all right, because of the magic.'

Mia shook her head. 'No. I don't have any. Unless – unless it's magic that I can be with you in dreams…?'

'Of course it is. How else do you think you were swimming under the water with us?' The mermaid looked scornful.

'I don't know,' Mia said humbly. 'I only thought I was dreaming. I did wonder if it might be the second sight – true dreams, I suppose. But I thought maybe it meant mermaids were real, not that I was actually there.'

The mermaid reached out one long-fingered hand – there were greenish webs between the fingers, Mia noticed, trying not to stare – and laid it on Mia's goose-pimpled arm. Mia flinched, just a little. Of course the girl had touched her before – she had dragged Mia all the way across the water – but this touch was different. It was determined, and it meant something.

The mergirl's fingers closed tighter on her arm, and for a moment she looked frightened. 'How can you think you don't have magic?' she muttered. 'It's everywhere inside you. But there's a skin over it. Don't you use it, ever?'

'No!' Mia snapped angrily. 'I don't have magic. It's my cousin – she's the magician. I'm not like her at all.'

The mermaid put her head on one side. 'You don't get to choose, you know.' She pricked Mia's arm with her sharp nails, and a faint sheen of water magic spread over her skin, cool and delicious. It should have made Mia feel colder, but instead something inside her seemed to glow. Her blood raced and she felt dizzy, as though she'd been spinning around and around inside the water chambers, laughing and twirling with the horses. Something of that happiness came back, from before she'd known what she was. The memory seemed to warm her from the inside out. 'You don't choose whether or not to have magic. It's just there, or not,' the mermaid said, gazing down at Mia's hands. 'Look.'

Mia looked down too, and swallowed. Her hands were golden – only faintly. If it had been sunnier, she would have said it was just the light. But it wasn't. She was glowing.

'Is that me?' she whispered.

But she knew the answer, even before she saw the mermaid roll her eyes. The golden light felt part of her. It felt right. Mia bit into her bottom lip, and she was silent for a moment.

'But I did choose,' she added slowly, thinking it out. 'When I was so angry with Olivia, when I first found out what had happened to my family. I refused to let magic have any part of me, so I couldn't be as hard and cruel as her. I didn't understand what I was shutting away...' She flexed her fingers, smiling at the shimmering light. 'I shut this away,' she murmured. 'Stupid...'

'Very,' the mermaid agreed. 'But powerful. So powerful that I still can't see how you did it. If you shut that away inside you for years, who knows what you've built up. It's no wonder you can dream-walk. Who's Olivia?'

Mia looked up at her in surprise. 'Don't you know? The duchess – my cousin.'

'Oh, well. If you're royal, that explains the magic.

What did this cousin do to make you hate her so much? Is that why you were going to walk into the water?'

'Don't you know anything about the city?' Mia asked curiously.

'We knew the magic was better.' The mermaid nodded. 'You stopped fighting with the sea, and we saw the horses more. They'd spent so much time sleeping, and then all at once it seemed as though they'd woken up again.'

'My cousin.' Mia kicked at the shallow puddle around her toes. 'She did it. She found a water horse and made him speak to her. It's a famous story now. And then he rescued her when my mother – her aunt – tried to take over the throne.' She glanced sideways at the mermaid. She'd never met anyone who didn't know this story before. The mermaid didn't even look all that interested, and Mia frowned. 'Mama did it because Olivia's father was dying, and she thought Olivia wasn't strong enough to be the duchess,' she went on, still watching the mermaid for a reaction.

But the girl twitched her shoulders in the growing sunlight, and flicked her tail. 'She was doing it to save the city,' Mia added, more urgently.

'Oh…' The mermaid brushed a smear of sand off a glittering scale, and smiled to herself.

'Don't you even care?' Mia burst out angrily.

'Well, it doesn't really matter, does it? Up there – we don't take that much notice of it.'

'You'll have to, when the Talish come,' Mia snapped. She looked at the mermaid, her skin gleaming in the faint sun that was starting to glitter over the lagoon, and her anger faded. What would happen to her and her sisters, and whatever else was far down in the water? The Talish wouldn't stop with the horses, once they knew there was power to be found. Mia was sure of that. 'Can you go deeper down?' she asked suddenly. 'Can you hide? And maybe take the horses with you?'

The mermaid shook her head. 'The horses belong in the city. They aren't sea creatures, not like us. Marsh-beasts, that's all.' She flicked her tail again, glancing smugly at the rainbow spray she made. 'Who are these Talish? Why do you want to hide us all away?'

Mia frowned, trying to think of a way to explain to someone who lived under the water. Maybe mermaids didn't know what wars were. 'They're a mighty army,' she said slowly. 'They want Venice to belong to them. The Emperor – their leader, you see – wants my cousin to marry his son.' She leant closer to the mermaid. 'And that sounds nice, but it's only because the wedding will make it look as though we don't mind that the Talish are in charge, and Prince Leo is just – just helping. But actually they're going to take over the city. And I think it's mostly because they're scared of our magic. The water magic that Olivia has, they want to crush it down and make it theirs instead.' She looked pleadingly into the girl's dark eyes. 'Don't you see? When they come, they'll start with the horses. I know Olivia will try to stop them, but once they're in the city, I don't know how she can. There's so much magic in the canals, and even in the buildings, the stones are full of it. But they won't stop. If they know about the horses, they'll look deeper, and they'll find you. And then the other things – there are other things, aren't there? I've seen them too.'

The mermaid blinked at her silently, and Mia's face twisted in a sad smile. Finally, she'd found a way to get the mergirl to pay attention. She wished she hadn't.

'You think they'll come for us?' the mermaid said at last.

'Yes.' Mia turned to look over her shoulder at the horizon, squinting against the rising sun. Were those black dots the ships? Or just the strong light blotching her eyes? She pressed the heels of her hands into her eyes and looked again. They were there – she could see the masts. 'They *are* coming. Look.'

The mermaid narrowed her eyes and peered into the sun, where Mia was pointing. She hissed a little at the brightness – Mia supposed she wasn't used to it, living down in the greenish depths. 'The shadows,' she muttered. 'The dark shadows, we call them that. So they're ships…they look like shadows to us.'

Mia nodded. They would, looking up from underwater.

'Is that why you were going to walk into the water?' the mermaid asked, turning suddenly back to Mia. 'Because you're afraid of these Talish?'

Mia shook her head. 'I am afraid,' she whispered. 'But I'm more afraid of me than I am of them. I'm afraid of what I might do.' She swallowed, and stared at the black ships. Was she imagining it, or had they moved closer? 'My mother is with the Talish, I think. I haven't seen her for seven years, since she was exiled and I was left here.' She squeezed her hands into fists. 'I want her back! It would be so easy… I'd only have to tell them what I know, and the ships would sail into the lagoon, and I'd be with her again. She'd be so pleased with me. But then…I really would be a traitor, like everyone thinks I am…'

The Talish would take this mermaid too, she thought. This strange, rude red-haired girl in the water who'd broken all the rules of her people because she couldn't bear to let Mia drown. She had to let her mother sit out there in her painted stateroom – she had to do everything she could to send her mother and Zuan away for ever.

So that she truly would never see them again.

'I want to be with her, but I can't,' she added miserably. 'I won't say anything. They'd come after you. It would all be spoiled, everything I dreamed.' She shook her head. 'I'll just have to stay in the city and have everyone hate me, like they do now.'

'And if it comes to fighting?' the mermaid asked her sharply. She was leaning closer now, her dark eyes glittering as she stared into Mia's own. 'If we have to chase these invaders away from our sea, what will you do?'

Mia stared at her, caught by the dark reflections moving in the mergirl's eyes, like the slowly churning currents of the sea. 'I don't know,' she whispered back. Would she really have to choose a side? *Could* she fight against her own mother?

The mermaid's eyes held her, and Mia dragged her own away, ashamed. She knew that she could, and it hurt. She didn't remember her mother or her brother properly at all. Only the idea of them. All she really knew was the emptiness where they should have been. Her mermaid dreams were more real than any faint memories of her mother's embroidered dress. They weren't even dreams, she knew now! She had spent hours and hours under the sea, hiding behind the weeds and smiling shyly at this same red-haired girl and her sisters. They had been her older sisters too. They were much too old and grand to let her join their games, but they'd loved her. She'd seen them smiling at her, they'd laughed as they found out her hiding places, and caressed her cheek with their waterweed hair.

Mia couldn't remember playing with her older brother. Had she, ever? As a little child she had played with the horses, but never with Zuan. She thought of the horses, dancing with her in the water chambers, and sighed. It wasn't her mother's fault, but those memories were stronger than any Mia had before the exile.

'You,' she muttered, pressing her face into her knees. 'I'd fight for all of you.'

CHAPTER FIVE

THERE WAS NO ANSWER – only a faint hiss of scales on sand, and then the salty smell of the mermaid's hair as she leant closer. 'I believe you would,' she said at last, wrapping her arms around the shivering girl.

They sat for a while, Mia leaning against the mermaid's shoulder, the hair tickling her cheek.

'The sun's getting higher,' the mermaid said, glancing around them. 'I'll have to take you back. I have to go.'

'What are you going to do?' Mia asked wearily. 'Can you warn the others? Will you go somewhere safer? You need to be where they can't find you.' She wanted to ask, *Will I ever see you again?* But she didn't think she could bear to hear the answer.

'I don't know what we'll do.' The mermaid sighed, and Mia felt the whisper of her breath like water lapping against a boat. 'I'll go back and talk to my sisters. Perhaps I can persuade them to help, somehow.'

'But how? You can't tell them about me – you said you weren't allowed to talk to us. What if they hurt you?' Mia pulled away a little and caught the girl's web-fingered hand, tugging at her to make her listen.

'I'll say I saw the ships and went spying by the palace to see if I could find out what they were. I heard people talking, that's all.' The mermaid hugged Mia tighter. 'It could almost be true. I'd looked for you before, you know. I even swam up one of the canals once, to see if I could tell which little land girl you were.'

'What's your name?' Mia whispered.

The mermaid hesitated for a moment, and Mia wondered if she wouldn't say – if her name was a secret, a spell of its own that would bind her if she told. But then the mermaid pulled away and held Mia at arm's length, looking into her eyes. 'Ara,' she said quietly. 'You?'

'Mia.' There was a lot more of her name than that, a string of jewelled names and titles, but Mia didn't think it mattered. 'Will you come back?' she added in a rush. 'Will you tell me what you're going to do?' Then she shook her head. 'No, you'd better not. It's too dangerous. You might be caught.'

Ara smiled at her, but the smile was grim. 'I *am* coming back, because we need you, and your magic. All the things that you know.'

Mia nodded, and then she ducked her head, shamefaced. 'But my magic only worked because you found it inside me. I still don't know how it works – what use can I be?'

Ara frowned at her, and flicked her tail through

the shallows. Then she flung herself off the sandbank, into the deeper water. She reached out her hands to Mia and Mia scrabbled after her, wincing and shuddering as the colder, deeper water swirled around her again.

'Kick,' Ara said, slipping back a little so that Mia had to follow her, reaching anxiously for her hands. She couldn't reach! 'That's it. And part the water with your hands.'

'I can't!' Mia felt herself sinking, dragged down by the weight of her nightgown, and she spluttered and panicked as her face dipped into the water.

'Try!' Ara hissed. 'Remember your dream – swim!'

It was only a dream, Mia wanted to say. *It wasn't real – I can't swim like that now.* But she was spitting out seawater, and she couldn't speak. She fought the water, slapping at it. She could feel it tugging her down, slow and inexorable, and she looked pleadingly at the mermaid, so close beside her but just out of reach. Ara shook her head, and only beckoned.

Mia felt the water she'd swallowed burning in her

chest, and she coughed again, suddenly angry. How dare Ara abandon her like this? She hit the water harder, striking it with the full force of her fear and fury – and it moved. Mia moved too, towards the mermaid, and Ara was laughing, and Mia wasn't choking any more.

'You see?' Ara grabbed her arm. 'You swam, just for a moment.'

'Was that my magic?' Mia gasped back, as Ara pulled her towards the city.

'A little magic, maybe. Or perhaps you were just swimming. But you did it, when you said you never could. So now remember. You can go back to your pretty palace and make your magic work, for when we need it.'

Mia nodded. 'I will,' she muttered hoarsely. Ara had sworn to her that the magic was there – she had felt it herself, that glowing, dizzy warmth. She would need it if she had to fight to protect her city, and the water.

'It's busy,' the mermaid whispered as they made

their way back between the morning traffic of the lagoon. 'Take a breath.'

'What?' Mia gulped air anxiously, and then tried not to scream as Ara dragged her underneath one of the palace skiffs, a light rowing boat piled with velvet cushions. *I should be there*, Mia thought wildly, as her chest burned and bubbles of precious air slid out of her mouth. *I should be leaning back on those cushions, watching the oarsmen.* She could see, in the darkness. Only a little, but enough to know when they were coming back out of the water. Her eyes stung with the salt, and she was growing dizzy for lack of air. And then they surfaced and she leant against Ara's shoulder, gasping, her lungs burning. 'Don't do that! I don't belong in the water!'

'Sssshh! Be quiet! Don't scream.' Ara clapped her hand across Mia's mouth and Mia fought the temptation to bite her. 'You'd better not,' the mermaid hissed, staring into Mia's furious eyes. 'We're here. Climb onto the island, quickly!'

She meant the floating floor of the pavilion, but

Mia was too tired and breathless to correct her. 'Please come back!' she gasped, as Ara disappeared in a weed-like swirl of red. But only a few bubbles floated up to answer her.

Mia sat at the edge of the pavilion, exhausted and shivering. How long had she been gone for? An hour, perhaps more? The palace would be busy by now. And she was soaking wet. Wearily, she got up and fetched her robe and slippers from the chest, wrapping herself in the fine brocade. The robe hid her wet nightgown, but her hair was trailing down her back in rats' tails, and she would have to walk back through the palace to her room in her nightclothes.

There was a stirring in the water, just beyond the pavilion, and Mia flinched. One of the water horses! She had been lucky that they hadn't arrived before. They would have been out watching the ships, she imagined. She looked wildly around, wondering if she should dart behind the chest again, but there was no time. A golden head was already emerging from the water, the horse whinnying and shaking cascades of droplets from its mane. It would see her, soaked and shivering, and the news would be with her cousin in minutes. Mia couldn't break the mermaid's secret, not yet.

She had wanted time to think about her magic – the terrifying knowledge that there was actually magic there, deep inside her. She had meant to circle round it, to tiptoe past and sneak glances, like a child creeping by a sleeping dog. But there was *no* time. The mermaids' secret was too precious – and if she broke it, Ara would be the one to suffer, not her.

If Ara hadn't spoken to her, Mia would have thrown herself into the water, and then who knew what could have happened? She had meant to drown. Perhaps the deeply-hidden magic would have broken out and saved her after all, but Mia hadn't known that – all she'd wanted was to escape.

There could be no gentle, careful trial of her powers now.

She closed her eyes, searching for that golden shell,

buried deep down, where Ara had found her magic. She thought of the water horse, so close, about to turn and see her any moment, and she tried to remember laughing and twirling and skidding through the water in this very room, before she had sealed her magic away. She had to summon it out of her, that same energy, the laughing lightness. She had shut it away with her power, when everything had seemed so dark and lonely. She wanted it back – she *needed* it back, now. The horse was stepping into the narrow channel that led back inside the palace. Any moment it would look around and see her, dripping wet, and smiling.

Mia felt the happiness burst deep down in her chest, like a mad laugh building up inside. She almost giggled – then the magic shimmered over her skin.

And she disappeared.

The water horse stomped past, snorting and shaking its silvery mane. It shied sideways as it stepped past the chest where Mia was standing – it couldn't see her, but perhaps it still knew that something was there? Stifling a giggle, Mia padded after it, dancing through the ripples the horse left behind. The creature whinnied and side-stepped, and Mia took pity on it, hurrying on past.

She padded quietly through the water chamber, dipping her feet into the glimmering shallows to see the water swirl, apparently all by itself. She chuckled delightedly to herself, looking back to see the damp footprints hurry up the marble steps and dance along the passageway. Then she snatched an apple from a tray carried by a passing serving boy. Once the apple was in her hand, it disappeared too, but the boy had seen it go. He gulped and hurried away, and Mia giggled, billowing the curtains with invisible fingers as she pattered past.

But as she came closer to her rooms, the strain of the magic began to tell. Each step grew heavier and harder to take. The spell flickered, and Mia saw her own wet slippers hurrying over the inlaid marble. She gasped and drew out more of the golden light, and she was gone again, but the spell was harder and harder to keep up. She dragged herself the last few steps, closing her bedroom door behind her with a soft click and leaning on it, fully visible again. Mia held out one hand, staring at her fingers. She felt so thin and misty she almost expected to see through them. The room seemed to whirl around her for a moment, and she pressed her hands gladly against the solid, comforting wood of the door.

Looking back, Mia was surprised she'd had the sense to change her nightgown and hide her water-stained things.

'It is very late. Are you awake, my lady?' someone whispered, and Mia blinked at one of her maidservants, peering round the bed curtains. She hadn't even heard the girl come in. She shut her eyes firmly.

'No. I'm ill, Maria. Leave me, please.'

'A posset, my lady? A hot brick to warm your toes?'

'No. I'm very ill. I feel most contagious, Maria. Go!' It was almost true. Mia felt exhausted – and so confused. What had happened? Dream-like images flittered through her mind, and Mia pressed her hands against her temples, shaking her head as if to scatter them away. 'Go!' she snapped again, as the maid still lingered at her bedside, clutching a silver tray of chocolate and sweet biscuits.

The maid squeaked nervously and hurried away, and Mia curled herself wearily into her pile of pillows. Had she truly seen a mermaid? Mia frowned to herself. She had definitely been in the water, but perhaps she had only dreamed the rest. It had seemed so real, but...

She sighed sadly into the feathery mass. She had been dreaming it for years. Of course it was a dream. It had been such a *nice* dream. So real, and even funny now, the way Ara was so sharp-tongued. Not like she'd imagined her at all...

Mia sat up again, frowning. The spell! She knew that was true – she could feel the magic inside her even now.

She reached up tiredly, wondering what it was that had caught in her hair – something hard, pressing against the pillows. She pulled at it, but it was caught fast, and she sat up with a sigh, reaching for the little hand mirror on the table by her bed. Mia gave a tiny shudder of disgust. Perhaps a crab had caught in her hair when she had fallen in the water – because of course, that was what must have happened. She peered cautiously into the mirror, hoping it was only a clump of seaweed, perhaps a few mussel shells.

Her hair was sticky with salt and her face was pale, smudged with shadows around her eyes. She *did* look ill. But wound in her salt-crusted hair was a comb, carved from mother of pearl. Tiny shells were set into it, and pieces of coral, even a lump of polished driftwood. It was as though someone had wandered across the sea bed, picking up pretty things, and then woven them all together to wear in their hair.

Mia ran her fingers over the gleaming shell surface and the weariness seemed to melt away.

How could she have thought that Ara wasn't real?

It was true, all of it.

The mermaids were real, but so were the dark

shadows, the great ships, sailing in to change and destroy everything they knew.

She got up later in the day, not because she wanted to – she still felt as though using the magic had worn her paper-thin – but because she didn't want anyone to ask awkward questions. Least of all her cousin, who would be almost sure to see the magic inside her now. Mia couldn't bear to have it all talked over. How could she explain that she had been foolish enough to seal away her own magic for years, because she'd been angry? 'You were sulking,' she muttered to herself crossly, as she twisted the shell comb carefully into her hair. 'Like a silly little girl.'

She felt stupid, and angry with herself, now that she realised what she had done and what she had given up – all because she had been so furious with her once-beloved cousin. She wasn't going to go running to Olivia now. She would just have to find out how to use the magic by herself. Besides, the secret of the mermaids wasn't even hers to share.

Mia lingered in her room, rather than parading in one of the galleries with the rest of the court ladies. It was safe enough – she often spent her days alone. Since Mia claimed that she was so broken away from the city's magic that she could no longer see the water horses, she could hardly go out to watch them playing in the lagoon as the others did most afternoons either. A few years before, she would have been one of the children of the city that the horses allowed to ride on their backs. A twinge of sadness pulled sharply inside her, thinking of the horses, and of one horse in particular, who had surely forgotten her by now.

Mia sighed, and went to the window, pushing sharply at the stiff iron frame so she could breathe the salty, fish-tinged smell of the water. The breeze was cool on her cheek, and all at once she couldn't stay indoors any longer. It was as though the water was suddenly hers again, after so long. She couldn't bear to stay away from it.

She turned away from the window and ran her fingers lovingly over the comb, still set in her hair.

She couldn't go back to the pavilion, not now. It would be busy with courtiers, admiring the water, and the horses. There would be too many watchers along the edge of the lagoon too. She needed a quiet, private patch of water. Somewhere she could dip her fingers in, and smile to herself and know that it had really happened.

Frowning, Mia padded to the door in silken slippers, wondering where she could go. It wasn't enough to dream of mermaids now. She wanted the silken cold of real water on her skin.

She stopped, her skirts swishing angrily, just before she reached the door. There *wasn't* anywhere. Every door out to the water would be guarded. People would see...

Mia nibbled at her thumbnail, staring doubtfully at the gilded door handle. Did that matter? There was a fleet of ships lurking at the entrance to the lagoon! Who cared if the ladies-in-waiting saw her by the water? Besides, it might be good to hear what everyone was saying about the Talish ships.

She nodded to herself, then stepped decisively to the door and flung it open, marching out into the corridor with tiny golden flares of magic streaming back from her like flags. She caught them back, pinching the magic away with her fingertips, and hurried down the passageway, smiling to herself. The magic wanted to show itself, now that she had set it free. If she wanted to keep her secret, she would have to be careful.

As she approached the grand staircase that led down into the main entrance hall, Mia set her face into its usual polite mask. She lifted her chin and armoured herself against the whispers. The knot of ladies at the bottom of the staircase were once again discussing her cousin and the Emperor's son.

'Think of the riches!' one of them twittered. 'The luxury! At least seven palaces. And she'll be an empress!'

An older girl shook her head. 'I don't think she should, however much they offer us. The duchess can't leave the city, surely? She belongs here, with us.'

'That's just some old superstition,' another of the girls jeered.

Mia had been trying to slip past without them noticing, but she caught her breath in a gasp at this. Of course it wasn't a superstition – didn't they understand how the royal family's magic was tied to the city? The girls turned at once to look at her, fixing on her like hunting birds.

'My lady!' One of the ladies-in-waiting, a dull, pale-faced, vicious girl, stepped towards her.

Mia smiled at her with an effort. 'Good afternoon, Lady Katarina. I thought I would walk by the water today.'

'By the water…?' Lady Katarina repeated, gaping a little.

'Yes. It's such a fine day, don't you think? I feel the need of some fresh sea air.' Mia swept past her, imagining the comb in her hair pulling her taller and straighter and grander than ever before. *I'm not afraid of you and your silly gossip. I swam with a mermaid.*

She stalked out down the steps of the palace,

breathing in the salt-laden air. She felt her step lighten, and her hair sprang into coils and danced around her in the breeze. She ran pattering in soft slippers over the marble flags to the side of the water, and stood balanced at the very edge. Out on the water she could see the horses, with laughing children diving around them, clinging to their manes and climbing over their smooth sides. She sighed a little, remembering.

'Lady Mia!' A gruff voice barked behind her, and she twirled unwisely on the edge of the water. She teetered a little, feeling the pull of the openness behind her, and the guard seized her wrist in his huge hand, dragging her back.

'Apologies, my lady. Would you have me call one of your maids? A lady-in-waiting?'

Mia blinked at him. 'Why?' she said at last.

The guard stared. 'You're alone, my lady. It...it isn't proper...'

'I'm footsteps away from the palace! Can't I look at the water in peace?' Mia took a slow breath and eyed him down her nose. 'If you are concerned, you may stand there and watch me,' she said coldly, turning her back on him again. But it was no good. With the guard standing there she couldn't trail her fingers in the water – let alone take off her embroidered slippers and dip in her toes, which was what she really wanted to do, even though it would ruin her silk stockings.

'Can you row a boat?' she demanded suddenly, turning back to glare at him. 'Please don't say *My lady?* as though you don't know perfectly well what I mean.'

The guard's mouth twitched. 'Yes, my lady. No, my lady.'

'Good. Then we will borrow one of the palace skiffs. I have a headache, due to the heat,' she added quickly. 'I only want to go out on the water a little way.'

The guard looked doubtful for a moment, but then he seemed to decide that an angry royal child was more dangerous than his watch commander. 'You wouldn't like me to fetch any of your ladies…?' he tried again hopefully. Mia didn't bother to answer. She simply stood by the mooring pole and glared at the looped rope until he handed her into the boat, and then untied it. For a moment he looked uncertain about what to do with his halberd – he could hardly leave it on the jetty.

'Lie it along the side,' Mia told him impatiently. 'Here.' She beckoned imperiously, snatching the heavy wooden pole as he lowered it towards her, and then gasping at the weight.

'Be careful, my lady,' he muttered, watching her anxiously, and then even more anxiously as he saw the halberd lighten in her hands.

Mia snatched at it, to stop it floating away. She wasn't exact with her power yet. Magic didn't seem to do as it was told. She refused to catch the guard's eye – at least now he was more likely to obey her orders. She could feel him watching her as he picked up the oars and manoeuvred them slowly away from the jetty.

'Where do you wish to go, my lady?'

'Anywhere...' Mia told him vaguely. 'Out onto the water. I need air, that's all.'

He rowed the slim wooden boat out, carefully avoiding the gondolas swarming past.

'Tie up here,' Mia told him at last, as they passed a line of boats moored to a buoy. 'We won't be long,' she added, seeing his worried glance back towards the palace. She leant over, folding her arms on the side of the boat and laying her head down to gaze into the water.

The guard shipped the oars and sat ramrod straight, arms folded. Mia supposed that he was still on duty. He couldn't let himself be comfortable. Gradually, though, the sun on the water and the soft lapping of the waves against the boat made his shoulders slump a little. Mia could feel her own eyes closing, and the water sounds began to merge into a sleepy whisper.

'Bewitch him...'

Mia shifted her cheek against her arm, blinking a little. She was half dreaming already, and the voice was so soft, so like the whispers of the sea, that she hardly heard it.

'Land girl! Mia! Send him to sleep!'

Her eyes flickered open, and this time she saw a flash of glistening red, like the gold and red china from the Orient that her cousin had displayed in one of the main receiving rooms. Mia blinked again and caught the ripple of sleep, sending it back across the water to lap at the guard instead.

She sat up a little, watching his head fall forwards, and then turned eagerly back to the water. 'Are you there?' she whispered.

The reddish glinting in the water grew clearer, and then Ara broke the surface, glittering drops flying out as she shook her hair.

'I couldn't believe that you were real,' Mia told her, rather shyly. 'I thought perhaps it was all just one of my dreams. I'm so glad you left me the comb.'

'I wasn't sure you would bring yourself to believe, unless you had something solid and real to touch. I saw you use your magic on the guard.'

Mia smiled, looking down at her hands. 'It feels so natural now,' she admitted. 'Strange, of course, and I don't know how to do anything with it. But it's part of me.' She glanced over at the guard anxiously. She had no idea how long the wave of sleep she'd washed over him would last, but he was snoring a little, his head slumped to one side.

'Did you go to look at the ships?' she asked Ara.

The mermaid shivered. 'Yes. There are so many. You said it was so, but to see them for myself…'

Mia nodded. 'Will you tell your sisters?'

Ara turned away, her pale shoulders hunched. 'I haven't yet. They won't believe me. They don't even believe it's happening, so they'll never agree to fight. I don't want to believe it either. This isn't our war, it's yours, the land creatures…' She shook her head miserably. 'How can I drag my sisters into the dark shadow of those ships?'

'I'm sorry,' Mia whispered.

The mergirl sighed. 'It isn't your place to be sorry. You are simply caught up in this as we are. Just pulled up in the net.' She laughed and reached up one cool, long-nailed hand to rest on Mia's. 'We're the little fish.'

Mia laughed too. 'Very little fish. Oh!' There was a grunting mutter from the other end of the boat and the guard shifted, yawning, and then cursing as he realised he'd slept. Then he straightened up at once, glaring suspiciously at Mia.

Ara swirled away with one last tight clasp of her fingers around Mia's. 'I'll see you again...' the ripples whispered, and Mia smiled. Then she nodded gravely at the guard.

'How strange! I must have fallen asleep in the sun. I apologise for keeping you so long away from your duties.' She folded her hands demurely in her lap. 'Perhaps now we should return to the palace?'

CHAPTER SIX

MIA YAWNED DELICATELY, HIDING her mouth with the back of her hand. She felt worn out, but not ill any longer. It was a healthy weariness, from being out on the water.

She sat by her window, sewing, although she set very few stitches. The sewing was just something to have in her hands, to help her think. She could hear laughter drifting round from the waterside, and she jabbed the needle into the ball of her finger and sucked at it, hissing at the sharp pain.

All the memories of the time before she had learnt of her mother's exile seemed so much stronger now. Perhaps it was because she had been out on the water again? She remembered the salty smell, and the way the wind would ruffle up the little cats'-paw waves out on the lagoon. She wanted to be out there again, even though swimming through the deep water had terrified her.

Mia threw down her embroidery and wrapped her arms tightly around her chest, thinking of that moment when she had been alone in the water, reaching for Ara. She had been so sure that the water would close over her face. Mia shivered, remembering the cold pull of the water, how easy it would have been to slip under. Only an hour or so before, that was what she had wanted to happen – or she'd thought she did.

When would Ara come to see her again? Mia wondered dreamily, leaning back against the cushioned chair. She had promised, but *when*? Remembering the undersea world of her dreams, she closed her eyes and tried to picture the mermaid, swooping and diving around the weeds, searching for more jewelled shells to make a comb.

The dream came to her quickly, as though it had been waiting to pounce. Mia had dreamed it so many times, always the same. She could see that little boat, silhouetted against the sunlight – but instead of standing on the jetty, this time Mia was watching from the water, shoulder-deep and clinging onto one of the wooden posts that held the walkway up. The tide was out and the posts were wreathed in pungent seaweed, and bunches of mussel shells.

Mia was so surprised at the changes in the dream that it took her a few seconds to see that she wasn't alone by the jetty. Ara was with her, diving in and out of the posts and then stopping by Mia's side to hold her hand. Mia squeezed it tightly and Ara kissed her cheek.

'Don't worry,' the mergirl breathed. 'I'll look after you.'

Mia smiled and nodded, and let go of the post,

following Ara out into the open water. The boat looked even further away now that they were watching from the sea. 'We can't swim after it,' she said sadly, and Ara shook her head.

Somehow, though, Mia didn't mind as much as she usually did. This time she didn't want to scream and beg for someone to bring her mother and Zuan back. They were gone, but she would not be alone.

But then the golden threads came, snaking along the surface of the water, as though they were woven from the sunlight dancing on the ripples. They wound around Mia's wrists, biting in tight. She gasped, plunging further down into the water as the cords tugged at her wrists. She kicked and struggled and strained her chin up, fighting to stay above the surface.

Ara cut through the water, back to Mia's side, and lifted her up, pulling her face out of the water. 'What is it?' she muttered. 'What are those things?'

'My mother,' Mia gasped. 'She doesn't understand. It's a dream, this is all a dream. The golden threads keep us together. They're to show she'll always love me.

I remember them from her dress. I always loved to look at the golden embroidery on her dresses. She doesn't understand what she's doing!'

But now the threads had loosened a little. They began to unwind themselves from Mia's wrists, casting around like dogs sniffing out their prey. A handful of glittering filaments snaked out through the water and sealed around Ara's wrist instead.

'They're trying to pull me away,' Ara cried, scratching at the cords with her claw-like nails. 'They want to pull us apart!'

'No…no, you don't understand,' Mia whispered. She wasn't sure if she was talking to Ara, or to the golden spell that was dragging her friend away. 'That's wrong. She's my friend. My mother sends the threads for *me*! This isn't what's supposed to happen! Please!'

But the threads were dragging Ara away from her in a frenzy of splashing. As the mermaid's fingers tore from hers, Mia felt the sudden weight of the gold threads around her arms – and the cold green water closed slowly over her face.

Mia woke the next morning still in her chair, frozen and aching. How had she spent the night here? Why had no one come to help her undress and get ready for bed? There was another grand audience with the Talish ambassador that morning – he was coming to present yet more gifts from Prince Leo, to pretend that the fleet of dark ships was a guard of honour, nothing more. The maids should have set out her dress, paraded past her with shoes and petticoats and jewels for her to approve.

Perhaps they'd tried, but she had sent them away again and not remembered? Mia rubbed wearily at her eyes. She felt worse than if she hadn't slept at all.

What had that dream been about? Why had the golden threads suddenly turned on her so mercilessly? The threads were her only true memory of her mother. She could picture the patterns of the embroidery so clearly, and she remembered tracing them with her fingers during the long court rituals, when she'd been a tiny child standing at her mother's side.

That dream had always been the same. Now it felt as though someone had come into her dream and snatched the memory of her mother away, it was unravelled, and broken. For a moment, Mia felt lonelier than she ever had before – and then she remembered that Ara had been there in the dream too. Ara had tried to save her.

Ara!

What had happened to her, when the golden threads dragged Mia away? When Mia had dreamed before, she had visited the mermaids under the sea – a dream for her, but true life for them. What if Mia's dream had hurt her friend?

Panicked, Mia patted at the skirts of her dress – was this what she had been wearing in the dream? The picture had seemed so clear, but in the strange half-real sense of dreams, Mia wasn't sure she had ever seen her clothes. Surely she couldn't have had this great heavy dress on in the water? And it wasn't wet, nor had it been wet, she decided, pressing the stiff silk between her fingers. It wouldn't have had time to dry, for a start. She took a deep, shaking breath.

Just a dream. Not real. But still…she had never thought her encounters with the mermaids were real either.

Mia sprang up out of her chair and ran out through the palace passageways to the water chamber. She didn't care who saw her as she went racing headlong down the marble steps to splash through the thin layer of water that had spread across the mosaic tiles with the high tide.

The silver mare that she had tried not to see for years woke and stared up at Mia as she dashed past. She whinnied sadly and laid her head down on her forelegs, as though she expected Mia to stare grimly straight ahead, as she always did.

It was Lorin's quiet sadness that caught at Mia's heart. The silver mare didn't even bother to speak to her any more – she knew it was no use. She'd spent years trying, after Mia suddenly stopped speaking to the horses. Whenever Mia had to come to the water chamber, or out by the lagoon, Lorin would be there, still hoping, standing close, silently pleading for Mia to see her, to speak.

Mia had wanted to, so much. She had been angry with Olivia – it had been easy to stop loving her – but Lorin and the other horses hadn't done anything wrong. Lorin had been her favourite, always, and then Mia had to tear herself away and pretend she wasn't there. It had been harder than anything.

But she didn't have to do it any more. With a sudden gasp Mia turned round, still half running. 'Lorin, I'm sorry!' she called.

As she turned back to dash out into the open air of the pavilion, she saw the horse gaze after her, her long silver-white mane coiling and tossing in excitement.

Lorin started to stand up, clumsy with sleep, and then Mia heard her call, 'I'll wait for you...'

At the edge of the water, Mia stopped, gazing out across the flatness of the lagoon. She should have asked Ara how to call a mermaid. Rather helplessly, she sat down on the edge of the platform, stiff and careful in her silk dress.

'Put your hand in the water,' someone murmured behind her, and Mia jumped, clutching at the wooden frame of the pavilion as she whipped round.

'I followed you,' the silver mare said apologetically. 'I know you said not to…'

Mia sighed. 'I probably would have followed me too. And it doesn't matter. It was because of a secret, but I don't think the secret's coming.'

The silver water horse lay down beside her, stretching her forelegs out into the sea. 'But that's what I said. If you want to call her, you need your hand in the water. Or your feet – but not in those.' She nosed Mia's delicate jewelled slippers. 'Too precious.'

'How do you know?' Mia stared at her. 'Did you *see*?'

The silver mare shook her mane and snorted a little. 'Of course I did. Do you think I don't watch you, still? I was here, sleeping. I heard you go by.

If the mermaid hadn't appeared, I would have stopped you walking into the water.' She nosed at Mia, nudging the girl gently with her velvet muzzle. 'You remembered my name all this time. I knew you had. I wouldn't let you drown.'

'I wasn't going to—' Mia started to say, but then she sighed and gave up. 'Had you seen the mermaids before?' she asked curiously. 'You don't sound very surprised. I didn't even know there was such a thing. Except in dreams.'

Lorin breathed out softly, leaning her great head down towards the water. 'Only glimpses. They live deeper out in the sea, and I like to swim further than some of us do. It may be that not everyone knows…' One soft nut-brown eye rolled sideways to peek at Mia. 'I am not – not very friendly,' she murmured.

'But you always were to me!' Mia said, surprised. 'You used to play with me.'

The mare said nothing, and Mia faltered to a stop. They were silent together, until Mia reached over to stroke the pinkish softness of Lorin's nose.

'I'm so sorry. I didn't know what I was doing. I did a lot of stupid things, I was so angry. I still am! And I was frightened,' she admitted. 'It felt as if I'd suddenly turned into someone else. Everything I knew had changed.'

'*I* didn't change!' the mare squealed, tossing her head away so that Mia cowered back against the floor, frightened of the great horse in a way she never had been before. But then Lorin settled back down, staring out to sea as though she couldn't bear to look at Mia.

'I know…' Mia whispered. 'You waited. All these years, when I never spoke to you and I even pretended that I couldn't see you. You didn't deserve that, not at all.'

The water horse said nothing, but her shining mane came coiling around Mia's shoulders, fragrant with salt and the freshness of a stiff breeze out on the sea. It was such a strange and yet familiar scent that Mia gasped and her eyes filled with tears.

'Why do you need the mermaid?' Lorin asked

gruffly, after a moment.

'I'm frightened for her,' Mia said, leaning against Lorin's silvery neck. The secret was out already – and Lorin had been her confidante all those years ago. She trusted the strange silver horse not to tell. 'I've had the same dream for ever, but last night it changed. Always before it was about my mother leaving, but she sent me golden threads that joined us together. This time Ara was there with me, and she never had been before. The threads didn't want her there, and they tried to pull us apart.' She shuddered, and the silver mare nuzzled her, pulling Mia close with her mane. 'They drowned me. And I don't know what happened to Ara.'

'But if it was only a dream…'

'I know – I know, it shouldn't matter, but I've had dreams about Ara and the mermaids before, and now Ara says that they were somehow real. She saw me, and she wasn't dreaming! It's something to do with my magic, she says, the way I closed it away inside me meant that I could walk in my dreams. What if this dream was half-real too? What if the magic hurt her?'

Lorin snorted, and nudged Mia's chin so that she turned to face the water. 'Look out there.'

Mia lifted her hand to shield her eyes from the bright sun, and gazed out into the water.

'There – between those two gondolas,' Lorin murmured.

All Mia could see was a clump of floating weed – but then she realised that the weed was what she was meant to see. Ara's glittering dark eyes met hers, and then the mermaid swooped under the surface, cutting through the water towards them.

CHAPTER SEVEN

'ARE YOU ALL RIGHT?'

'What happened?'

Both girls spoke at once, and Mia leant down to hug Ara tightly. Then she sat back, suddenly shy. Whenever they had touched before, Ara had made the first move – would the mermaid be offended? Mia had just been so glad to see her.

But Ara rested her elbows on the wooden floor and smiled at her, looking almost as shy as Mia felt. 'What were those things?' she demanded.

'So you dreamed it too?' Mia asked slowly. 'The golden threads?'

Ara wrinkled her nose. 'I don't know if I was dreaming or not … I think I was inside *your* dream. I could see that it wasn't real – I could break out, back into the undersea. But I couldn't take you with me.' She caught Mia's hand. 'I did try! I scratched and clawed at the threads, but they wouldn't tear, and the more I dragged at them the weaker you seemed to get. Then they pulled you under the water and everything went dark for a moment. After that I was on my own again.' She bit her lower lip, her sharp teeth pressing hard into the skin. 'I thought you were dead.'

'When I was in the dream, I thought I was too,' Mia whispered back. Lorin nuzzled against her, and the salty coils of her mane spread round Mia's shoulders. 'This is Lorin,' she told Ara. 'She's…' She looked round at the water horse, and found Lorin's dark eyes fixed on hers. 'She's my oldest friend. But I'd almost forgotten her – the water horses were all tied up with the magic, for me.'

Ara dipped her head, a slow, formal nod to another water creature. 'My lady,' she murmured. Then she turned again to Mia. 'It can't have been only a dream. You said something about your mother. That she sends those things.'

Mia nodded. 'It's all I have of her now. Always before, the threads tied me back to my mother – they were the only way I could remember her. I can't understand why they've changed.'

Lorin looked from Mia to the mergirl, and then back again. She huffed a great hot breath out of her pinkish nostrils and Mia stared at her.

'What is it?'

'Your mother's magic was very powerful,' Lorin murmured. 'She was a great magician – stronger than your cousin Olivia in some ways. It was Olivia's love for the water and us horses that strengthened her.'

Mia nodded. 'I know. It must have been a very great spell, to make those threads last for so long. It's seven years since they left.'

Lorin sighed again. 'Mia, those threads are not just to remind you of your mother.'

Ara nodded. Her eyes looked darker than ever, wide and sorrowful, and Mia flinched. She wasn't sure what they were trying to tell her.

'It would explain why you could deny your own magic so easily, as well,' Ara said thoughtfully. 'I couldn't see how a child so young could make that happen.'

'What would explain it?' Mia asked, swallowing hard and forcing the words out.

'There's a spell on you – those golden threads are part of it.'

'But I know that!' Mia said, smiling in sudden relief. 'I told you that, that's what we just said,' she added impatiently. Why were they making such a fuss about it?

'It isn't just your mother trying to send you her love, Mia.' Ara caught her hands. 'It's more than that. She's *binding* you.'

'That spell has you under her control,' Lorin agreed.

'Not a very strong control – not yet, anyway. But it's there, and as soon as the spell sensed that there was another influence on you, it tried to break you apart.'

'What other influence?' Mia demanded.

'Her.' Lorin flicked her ears at Ara.

Mia almost laughed. Ara's face changed, and her shoulders stiffened – suddenly she looked haughty. Obviously it was beneath her dignity to be called 'her' by a horse. But now there was a deep, scared pit inside Mia's stomach and she was too frightened even to smile. 'Wouldn't I know if I were under a spell?'

Ara shrugged and Lorin tossed her mane. 'Maybe, maybe not,' the water horse said. 'I don't think you've done anything that would make the spell fight you, until now, you see.'

'But why would she?' Mia cried. 'She isn't even here, so what's the point of...' But her voice trailed away as she remembered what the world said her mother had done. Everything she had been working for had been taken away – and her daughter had been taken away from her too. Perhaps Lady Sofia had seen an opportunity. She'd tried to leave the last part of her plan in place with Mia.

'But that means the council are right,' she said slowly, trying to think it out. 'I *am* a traitor, just like my mother was. All this time I was so angry with my cousin for sending her away. I was sure that it wasn't fair, and my cousin was just being cruel. And it turns out that my mother was even worse than Olivia thought. Have I been under a spell ever since I was born?' Mia swallowed painfully. 'Didn't she ever love me just for me? It feels as if I was only ever meant to be part of some terrible plot...'

'We don't know she means you to hurt the city. You haven't done anything yet,' Ara pointed out, squeezing her hand.

'I could, though, any moment. And what if I have done something awful and I don't even know it?' Mia snatched her hands back from Ara and stared at them in horror. 'It could be anything!'

'Perhaps to you it might feel like a dream,' Lorin said thoughtfully.

Ara swirled suddenly in the water, the muscles of her tail twisting. 'Yes! Dreams, of course!'

'What?' Mia asked fearfully.

'The dream magic,' Ara murmured. 'I thought you could walk in your dreams because you'd hidden your magic away, and it had grown so strong. But it didn't explain what was happening – how you were doing something so strange. Don't you see? If your mother's spell sets you to work in your dreams, and she uses them to reinforce her spell, that would be why. Your magic is drawn to dreams now. Your dreams are real.'

Mia frowned down at her hands, twisting and turning them in her lap, as though she might find some kind of clue in the lines on her skin. 'So because my mother's spell works through dreams, that meant I could visit you under the sea.' She smiled a little. 'At least some good came out of it, then... I hope that stays, when I break the spell.' She glared at the two water creatures, both watching her with pity in their eyes. 'Because I *will* break it. I don't care how great a magician my mother was. She doesn't know *me*. I've already done something she doesn't like by meeting you, Ara. She sent her golden threads to tear us apart, but it didn't work.'

The mermaid nodded. 'And her own spell brought about our meeting under the sea – it shows she can't be controlling everything you do, or the way you think. She can only use your dreams to steer you from a distance.'

Mia shuddered. 'It's so strange – I feel as though I have to question everything I've ever done now. Was it me, or was it the spell? Did she want me to give up my magic? Is that why I was so angry with Olivia and everything to do with the water?' She looked miserably at Lorin. 'Did she make me give you up, or was I just being stupid?'

Lorin snorted, a low, bubbly laughing sound. 'Who knows? But I suspect that the way you turned your back on everything magical was down to you yourself. Wouldn't your mother have wanted you to grow up knowing your magic? Wouldn't you be stronger now if you'd been taught?'

Ara shook her head. 'It could have been. Perhaps she did see how much you were growing to love the water horses, and she thought she needed to drag you away. She didn't know that by making you so lonely, she'd cast you into a dreamworld. It stole you away from her even more than Lorin had. Besides,' she added to Lorin, 'if Mia knew more about how her own magic worked, she might be able to break out of this spell.'

'I'll break it anyway,' Mia muttered. 'If I have to read every book on magic in my cousin's library.'

'You could ask her to help you,' Lorin suggested, but Mia looked at her in horror.

'Of course I can't! She already thinks I'm – I'm *suspect*. And I am,' she added miserably. 'She might even send me away to Talis.' Mia laughed bitterly. 'And a few days ago, that was exactly what I wanted. How can that be? Everything's turned upside down.'

Lorin scrambled up, glittering droplets of water cascading from the white fringes round her fetlocks. 'Someone's coming.'

'My cousin?' Mia gasped, jumping up too. 'Ara, goodbye! Will you come back tomorrow morning? Early, like today? We haven't even spoken about the ships, or about your sisters. But the Talish are still trying to persuade my cousin to marry Prince Leo. There's another audience today. There's still time.'

'I'll come, or you can call me like before – remember, you must be touching the water, like Lorin said.' Ara disappeared in a little eddy and Mia scrambled away from the waterside, running headlong through the pavilion and into the palace itself. There she darted behind a latticed screen until the little party of courtiers had made their way past to look out at the water and the menacing line of dark ships across the horizon.

'I wish you could come back to my rooms with me,' she said to Lorin, as she slipped out from behind the screen. 'If I stay here, someone's bound to notice me and ask questions.' She wound both her hands into Lorin's mane and sighed. 'Perhaps I could come back tonight, late. Would the other horses notice?

Would they tell my cousin?'

'What if they do?' Lorin snuffled at her cheek. 'Could you not let your cousin see that you know me again now? Does it really matter?'

'No. It doesn't. I shall tell her soon.' Mia turned and kissed Lorin's muzzle. 'Just – not quite yet. Not until I've had a chance to see what this all means.' She shivered. 'That sounds so devious. I suppose my mother must have considered things the same way… Perhaps I'm more like her than I want to be. I must go – the Talish ambassador is presenting another round of gifts this morning, and it'll take hours to be properly dressed. It will be in here, I think, so I shall see you, even if we can't talk.' Reluctantly, she unwound herself from Lorin's mane, stroking the warm coils – they were looped around her wrists like her mother's golden spell, but they felt so different. She stepped away from the silver mare and then ran back, throwing her arms around Lorin's powerful neck one last time. 'I'll never, never abandon you again,' she whispered.

The presentation in the water chamber was even more strange and stiff than the court events usually were. Now, when visiting nobles asked who the pale-faced girl standing close to Her Grace's throne was, Mia knew that all the nasty gossip the court ladies were passing on was actually true. She tried to close her ears to it, as she always did, but it seemed that every stray word she heard had some horrible significance.

The Talish ambassador had brought another portrait of Prince Leo, this one enclosed in an exquisite jewelled locket, which he invited Her Grace, in the most flowery language, to put on at once. Somehow he managed to imply – without ever actually coming out and saying so – that if she did not put the pretty jewel around her neck, the ships would be sailing into the lagoon within days.

It was all very difficult to bear. Mia had spent the last few years wishing she didn't have to attend these events, or at least that she didn't have to stand so close to her cousin. Now, she wanted nothing more than to shake Olivia and tell her that she mustn't even consider saying yes, or the Talish would plunder every last scrap of magic from Venice and her waters.

Looking at her cousin, though, Mia was almost sure that she already knew. Her face was white and thin, and there were purple smudges under her eyes. The water horse who was her closest companion, Lucian, was standing next to her throne. He towered over her, hugely muscled at the shoulders, and it was very clear that he objected strongly to the Talish ambassador's veiled threats. He kept stamping his great hooves and snorting.

The ceremony involved a choir, apparently trained by the prince himself. They sang of his infatuation with the beautiful duchess (whom he'd never met) at great length. There were also a good many speeches, from both sides. And then there was a formal meal that lasted late into the evening. Mia dragged herself back to her room feeling unpleasantly sick, since out of politeness she'd had to taste every course.

Once the maids had helped her out of the stiffly corseted dress and helped her to arrange a lace-trimmed robe, Mia dismissed them, pleading tiredness after the ceremony. She wanted to rest, she said, her fingers itching for them to be gone.

She *was* tired – she had been smiling sweetly for hours – but she was not going to *rest*. She was going to investigate this spell, this deceitful chain that had been ruling her life for so long.

The problem was, Mia realised, as she stood in the centre of the room, listening to the voices of the maids as they hastened away down the corridor, that she had no idea where to start. She had used her magic by instinct, to stop herself from drowning and to make herself disappear that one time, and since then only for a couple of tiny charms. They had been almost accidental – because she needed them. There had to be other ways to call the power up, but she had no idea what they were.

She would start with a proper spell – she might never have repeated one herself, but she had heard them spoken. Surely a few words would be enough to waken the power inside her, even if she didn't actually make anything happen?

Mia shivered, remembering Signor Jac, his white face and dark, glittering eyes. The magic was the first thing anyone noticed about her cousin's councillor. He wore it around himself like a cloak, spilling out of him as though he couldn't hold it back. Setting her shoulders back, Mia tried to mouth a few of the words she had heard him mutter – but they sounded lifeless and flat in her nervous little voice, and she knew that they were useless.

She wanted her fingers to glow with that warm light again, the way they had when Ara showed her the magic she'd been hiding. She needed the dancing excitement shining out of her skin! But when she looked down at her hands, they were thin and soft and white. The only tasks they could do were embroidery, or perhaps holding a book, when she could be bothered to study. Mia tried to remember them glittering with magic, but they looked so feeble and pasty she couldn't see them as the same hands at all.

She tried again, and again – striding up and down the room, waving her arms in great, wild gestures. No hint of magic blossomed inside her. At last she stopped, panting in the shadowy room. Hours had passed, and she hadn't even felt a spark.

'How am I ever going to find it?' she muttered to herself, shaking her fingers, as if the magic might fly out. 'I've spent all this time hiding it from myself.' She pressed her hands flat against her ribs, trying to work out where that golden sense of magic had been hidden. All she could feel was her own breathing, slow and regular. Snarling to herself, Mia flounced into a chair. She wouldn't go crawling to Olivia, she *wouldn't*.

Wearily, she pressed her hands into her eyes, so hard that she saw stars in the darkness. She couldn't give up.

Then the darkness became laced with gold, and Mia's breath caught in her throat. She dragged her hands away from her eyes, wrenching them open. But still all she saw was darkness and gold. A heavy rich gold, like the embroidery on her mother's dresses. It clung tightly around her, pushing and shaping her, the way it had always done. She tried to lift her hands, to scratch away the golden binding from her eyes – but they lay weakly in her lap, not even twitching. Had her mother felt her trying to wake her magic? Perhaps she realised that there was only a little more time to use her last chance to work against Olivia.

Mia tried to scream, to beg for someone to call Lorin, or even her cousin. She wouldn't care – she would tell Olivia what had happened. It didn't matter! But instead of crying out, she stood up – or something stood her up. The golden threads pulled on her like a loose-limbed puppet and began to walk her across the room.

There was something in the pocket of her lacy robe, she realised, as her numb fingers fought with the fastening of the door. Something heavy, something that shone in the lamplight, glinting through the open pattern of the lace. Something awful. She was going to do something awful – the spell, her own mother's spell, would make her do it.

The heavy, shining thing banged against her leg as she walked up the corridor to her cousin's rooms and smiled sweetly at the guard. He had known her since she was a tiny child, and he didn't expect the glittering threads that Mia's hands cast into his eyes, leaving him writhing on the cold marble floor.

Mia slipped through the door, and another, and another, until she was standing just inside her cousin's bedchamber, the thing in her pocket – the *knife* – now in her hand. Olivia was sleeping in her great carved bed, a tiny, fragile mound under her lace comforter.

Mia's hand tightened on the gleaming metal in her pocket. Her fingers fumbled over it – and then stopped. They were rigid, the joints pressed against the skin with the whiteness of bone as Mia fought the spell.

'I won't,' she whispered. The spell was fighting her

hands, she realised slowly. Her head felt as though it was filled with mud, or molten metal. Something dark and syrupy that slowed her thoughts – but she *was* thinking for herself. The spell couldn't control all of her, it wasn't strong enough, and it was fighting her hands now, so she could still think, and talk.

'I could scream,' she whispered to herself. 'I should.' But then everyone would come running. They would find that poor guard, and she would be condemned. Exiled or imprisoned – taken away from Lorin and Ara, and the city.

But the spell seemed to draw back, just then, as though it dreaded the thought of discovery as much as she did, and Mia felt it go. The glittering gold cast that had coloured the whole scene faded a little.

With a sudden force that almost pulled her over, Mia turned, yanking her body back into her own control and running headlong out of the room. She dragged the mass of golden wires from the guard's face as she dashed past, hoping that he wouldn't remember what had happened to him.

Or that he would believe it was a dream, and not want to admit that he'd been sleeping on duty. The golden stuff fizzed and coiled and turned to sticky dust as she ran away down the passage, making for the sea, and for Lorin and Ara. Mia flung herself down the steps into the water chamber and plunged her hands into the cool salt water over the marble floor, rinsing away her mother's unclean magic.

All across the dark room, pale heads lifted, and glimmering tails beat against the water, but Mia ran straight to Lorin. She didn't even wonder how she knew that Lorin was the silvery shape closest to the pavilion doors, even in the dark – she simply did know, and she needed her oldest, most patient friend. She had forgotten the dangers of the other water horses – she no longer cared.

She flung herself down in the water next to Lorin, folding her arms against the silvery coat and crying bitterly.

'What is it, what's happened?' Lorin murmured. And then, 'Ssssh, sssh, go back to sleep, I expect the child has had a bad dream. Leave her alone.'

Vaguely, Mia heard hooves splashing away, and then Lorin's warm, tickling muzzle was pressed against her ear. 'What has happened, Mia?'

'I had a knife! I was in her room! I was going to kill her!' Mia sobbed.

'But you didn't?' Lorin demanded quickly.

'Of course not – but I almost did.' Mia sniffed. 'I came so close, Lorin. I could hear her breathing. The knife was in my pocket – I must have picked it up from one of the trays they brought me. Who knows when I did that? I must have had it hidden in my room – hidden even from me!'

'Why did you stop?' Lorin asked.

Mia caught her breath mid-sob, trying to think. 'I don't know.' She lifted her head a little way off her arms. 'I didn't want to hold the knife...' she said slowly. 'I knew what I was supposed to do with it, and I don't want to hurt Olivia – not like that, anyway.' She laid her face down against Lorin's mane. 'I'd still quite like it if she was miserable.

I can't stop being angry with her, not all at once. I'm almost *more* angry now, because she was right all along, wasn't she? My mother was a traitor, and so am I.'

Lorin made a tiny snuffling noise. 'You think your cousin is happy?'

'I suppose not,' Mia muttered, feeling stupid. She'd stopped crying and her robe was uncomfortably damp. 'I have to get rid of this spell. I *must*. I only just managed to stop myself this time. What if next time it's stronger, or I'm asleep? I could do *any*thing.'

'I never thought your mother would expect you to kill,' Lorin whispered, her voice a low rumble.

Mia said nothing for a moment. 'Nor did I,' she whispered. 'I wished and wished that she'd come back. Or that she'd taken me with her in the first place. But now... Lorin, I don't think she cares about me very much. Not as her child. I suppose' – her voice shook a little – 'I suppose she hasn't seen me for seven years either. But I'm not sure she ever did care. I'm just a useful thing, for her. I'm convenient.'

Lorin nosed her gently. 'I want to say that you're wrong, but I would be lying to you, dearest.'

'Will you take me to find Ara? She's seen the spell in my dream, and she understands magic more than I do. Do you think that together the three of us could break it? I can't wait any longer, in case my mother makes it work the next time.'

'We can try.' Lorin sounded a little doubtful, but she shifted her hindquarters and nudged Mia again. 'Get on my back.'

Mia's heart jumped. 'Really?' she asked. It was so long since she'd ridden any of the horses. When she was little, she had bounced around on Lorin's back as if she was sitting on a great padded bench, clutching the long mane and squealing with delight.

She stood up and carefully swung her leg over, winding her fingers into the curls of Lorin's mane and laughing a little. There was a hollow, just behind the mare's shoulders – it was as if she was meant to be there.

'Oh, I love you...' she whispered. 'I still love you.'

She rested her head against the great silver neck for a moment, remembering, and then pulled herself up. She couldn't dream away this time in memories. 'Lorin, if we can't break the spell, will you do something for me? Will you take me far away from here, where my mother can't make me hurt Olivia, or any of you?' She hated to say it – it had been only that day she promised never to leave Lorin behind again. But she couldn't stay if she was going to hurt the water creatures, or anyone else.

The water horse stood up and reached round to nip sharply at the sleeve of Mia's robe. 'Be quiet, stupid child,' she muttered. 'It won't come to that.'

'But would you?'

'Yes,' Lorin muttered back. 'But I'd have to stay there with you. Now be quiet.'

CHAPTER EIGHT

M IA HAD NEVER BEEN out on the water in the
dark – at least, not without a torchlit
procession of gondolas, and a choir, and half the
court. Instead she was slipping through the dark
water on Lorin's back, watching the ripples glide
past them. The sea was calm and quiet, the only
sounds the faint slapping of the water against the
moored boats and an eerie thread of music from
one of the buildings across the water at La Giudecca,
on the opposite bank.

Lorin swam so surely that Mia realised she must be able to see in the dark. She cut swiftly around the boats and through the broad channel between the islands in the lagoon, Isola La Certosa and the Lido, out towards Sant'Erasmo, to look for the sandbar that Mia had told her about. 'We're almost there,' she murmured after a few more minutes.

All Mia could see were the dark bulks of the islands, blacker lumps against the night sky, jewelled with a few bright lights. She couldn't see the sandbar at all. But Lorin's water magic could clearly sense that the sea was growing shallow.

'Call the mergirl,' Lorin said, looking back over her shoulder, and Mia leant down, lying flat along Lorin's back and trailing her hand in the water.

'Ara!' she whispered. Mia spoke out loud but she had a sudden realisation that it wasn't *hearing* her call that brought the mergirl, it was more that she *felt* her call in the water. 'Ara, please, if you can hear us, come to the sandbar,' she called, stirring her hand in the water. Then she gasped, and tried to draw her hand out of the water so quickly that she almost slipped from Lorin's back. Another chill hand had slid from the water and gripped her own. 'Ara! You frightened me!' Mia gasped as the mermaid surfaced beside them in a swirl of reddish weed. Ara was smiling, and Mia could see the points of her teeth gleaming in the moonlight. 'You did that on purpose,' she murmured, as Lorin's swimming shifted and they came out onto the sandbank.

'I didn't mean to. Why didn't you call to me from the pavilion?' Ara asked, as she hauled herself up onto the sand after them.

Mia slipped down from Lorin's back and sat by Ara. 'Lots of the other horses were sleeping in the water chambers tonight. I couldn't risk anyone else overhearing. As it is, they know we've gone. I wouldn't be surprised if one of them tells my cousin, but it's too important now, I can't worry about that.'

'What's happened?' Ara stroked Mia's hair, patting the shell comb that was tucked above her ear.

Mia swallowed. It was so hard to say. 'I tried –
to stab Olivia…' she whispered. 'I almost did it.
I was trying to pull the knife out of the pocket of
my robe.'

Ara caught her chin, pulling Mia to face her. 'But
you stopped yourself? Or someone stopped you? Is
the duchess dead? I must warn my sisters, and the
creatures of the deeper sea. Those ships will be into
the lagoon in hours, if she is dead.'

'She isn't,' Lorin snapped. 'Mia broke out of the
spell. But we must remove it from her for good. We
can't let this happen again.'

'Very well.' Ara nodded, and Mia saw that she was
trembling. The news had shaken her.

'We will stop it somehow,' she said suddenly,
trying to reach out, to take Ara's hand, but the
mermaid shifted in the water, out of her reach. 'The
Talish ships – we won't give in. They won't take the
city and all of you. My cousin won't let it happen,
I promise.'

'My sisters don't understand,' Ara murmured,

dipping her head down so that she was hidden behind her fall of reddish hair, and Mia could hardly hear her. 'They say we must stay away, as we always have, and the humans won't trouble us. They don't understand!'

Mia sighed. 'How could they? But then that means they aren't going to do anything to protect themselves.' She looked at Ara, bent over hopelessly on the sand, and edged closer towards her. If the mermaids couldn't see the danger, it made them seem so vulnerable. 'Ara, if I can't undo the spell, I might not be properly me... I don't know if I can fight with you, even though I promised I would. What if my mother's spell makes me hurt someone? Please. You have to help me escape. Then I'll help you and your sisters, I really will.'

Ara tossed her hair out of her face and nodded wearily. 'I know. I'm sorry. I was just thinking of what might happen – there's no good in that. Was it the same spell?'

'It was the golden threads again. I saw them in

the darkness behind my eyelids. Like the marble floor in the throne room, all grey and black with gold streaks.'

'Marble…' Ara said thoughtfully. 'A black stone. There are many stones like that, on the sea bed. I wonder… Sometimes, with a spell, something to hold can be useful.' She flicked her tail and Mia saw the power of the great muscles underneath the glittering scales. The mermaid sprang into the air, pointing her hands like an arrow as she dived back, sliding just under the surface of the shallow water.

Mia smiled, but her smile was a little lopsided. She did that too – when she felt most desperate, when the whispers were all around her. That was when she stood straightest, and wore her best dresses. Ara was putting on a show.

The mermaid shot out of the water again, with a round black rock cupped in her hands, water-smoothed and glistening.

She handed it to Mia, and Mia shuddered as she traced the glittering threads of gold that tracked across the stone. 'It's so like what I saw. But I don't understand – can we use this somehow? It's nothing to do with my mother's magic.' She looked at it in sudden disgust, and tried to press it back into Ara's hands. 'It isn't, is it?'

Ara smiled, showing her sharp upper teeth. 'No, it isn't. Not yet. But you can feel it, can't you? You can't stand to hold it now! It makes you think of the spell – and if they're tied together in your head, we can tie them together for real.'

Mia frowned at her. 'I don't see how.'

'Like an amulet?' Lorin put in, peering at the stone. 'The magicians at the court have those, Mia. Little statues sometimes, or jewellery, with a scrap of magic in. To help with a particular spell.'

'Yes!' Ara nodded. 'But this should be the opposite. We don't want to build the spell – we need to draw it out of her.'

Lorin peered at the stone, her ears pricked forward. 'Will it really work?'

Ara shrugged her thin shoulders expressively.

'Who knows? But we can try.' She touched one finger to the stone and closed her eyes.

'What are you doing?' Mia gasped, as the stone grew warm and seemed to shake between her fingers.

'Putting some of my own magic in it.' Ara hissed with the effort. 'Like to like. Magic is attracted to itself. We want to charm the spell out of you and into the stone.'

Lorin lay down, curling herself around them like a mare with two foals, touching the dark pebble with her short, bristling whiskers. It made her shudder too. 'Even thinking of this as your spell makes it seem dangerous,' she said, drawing her head back. 'It smells sharp – it burns my nostrils, like a strong magic.'

Mia's fingers shook, and the golden lines seemed to glow with a fiery brightness as the three of them gazed at the stone. How could a small round pebble from the sea suddenly seem so malevolent?

'I hate you,' she muttered, squeezing the stone tight and wishing it was the spell she was hurting instead of her own fingers. 'Get away, get out. Leave me!' Her fingers itched to throw the stone away, and she raised her hand with a sharp gesture. But then there was a triumphant flare of gold in the corners of her eyes and Mia let out an angry snarl. 'It was tricking me,' she muttered. 'It wanted me to throw it away. But I can feel the spell inside me,' she added slowly, turning the stone over and over in her hands. 'It's as if I'm winding it up, like thread on a reel… But it's so hard to make it turn.' She gasped suddenly. 'It's pulling at me!'

Ara cupped her hands around Mia's and blew gently on Mia's pale fingers. Mia let out a tiny cry as another length of magic seemed to be teased out of the angry knot inside her and rolled into the stone.

'Is it hurting?' Lorin demanded anxiously.

'Yes – but I don't care, keep doing it,' Mia begged, squeezing her eyes tight shut. The magic was being dragged out of her bit by bit, and it felt as though half her insides were going with it. 'It's going, don't stop…'

But then that same blackness laced with gold began to cover her eyes again, and her hands sagged under the sudden weight of the stone. With a sigh, Mia slipped sideways, slumping against Lorin's side, unconscious.

Mia woke to find herself stretched out on Lorin's back, with a lock of the water horse's silvery mane wrapped tightly around her wrists – as though to stop her from sliding off. Lorin was lying on a beach, half-mud, half-sand, one that Mia didn't recognise.

'You're awake!'

Mia rolled over a little, and peered sleepily at Ara. The mermaid was lying beside Lorin, resting on her elbows, but now she sat up and caught Mia's hands.

'Did I sleep all night?' Mia murmured. The sky was pale and pink-streaked, and she guessed it must be just before dawn.

'We didn't know if you were asleep – or something else. We called you and shook you, and begged you to talk to us, but your eyelids didn't even flicker. So we brought you here, further away from the city, in case we needed to hide for a while.'

'What happened to the stone?' Mia asked, unravelling Lorin's mane from around her wrists and sitting up slowly. Lorin yawned and thumped her tail into the water, and a shower of chill spray spattered on Mia's face and shoulders. She shivered, but she felt more awake.

'You don't know?' Ara reached down to the sand beside her and held out to Mia the gold and black stone – or rather, stones. The black stone had split in half, with what looked a terrible force. Instead of splitting cleanly, it had broken in great jagged spikes. But in the centre of both halves was a nugget of reddish-golden metal.

'Is that the spell?' Mia asked, putting her hands behind her back. 'No, I don't want to hold it. What if it tries to get back inside me?' She peered at the darkly gleaming metal. 'Do you think that's all of it?' She squinted sideways for a moment, and then laughed, looking a little shamefaced. 'I think I was trying to see inside my own head,' she explained, pressing her hands against her temples. 'It aches so.'

'Do you feel as though it's gone?' Lorin asked, lipping gently at Mia's hair.

'I can't tell,' Mia sighed. 'Especially since I didn't know it was a spell in the first place. I can't see anything glittering. But the rest of me looks just the same as it always did. Except...' She frowned, flattening her hands against her ribs. 'I feel lighter, here. As though...' Mia stretched one hand, sucking in her breath at the effort it took just to make that simple gesture. Fighting the spell had exhausted her. She chewed at her lower lip and swooped her hand around, laughing a little at that joyful sense of lightness inside her, even though she felt so desperately tired.

A tiny spout of water twirled up out of the sea, shadowy and grey in the pre-dawn light. It danced over the surface of the water and swirled around their feet, chittering to itself, with the sound of a stream running over stones. The water sprite ran over Ara's hands and seized the black stones, which sat hulking in the mermaid's grasp like a toad. It bore the stones away inside itself, and disappeared down into the depths of the sea with a satisfied little splash.

'Hm.' Lorin sniffed. 'A good first use of your magic, I suppose. But you had better hope that no poor fisherman brings that up in his nets.'

'I didn't think of that,' Mia said, looking worriedly at the faint ripples in the water.

'It's in two pieces,' Ara pointed out. 'The fisherman would have to be very unlucky to catch both of them.'

'It's such a beautiful morning,' Mia said quietly, stepping down off Lorin's back and peering up at the chilly pale sky. 'Or it will be. But there's something…odd. Don't you feel it? Something different.'

'Perhaps you really have got rid of all of the spell,' Ara suggested hopefully.

'No…it's not that. It's almost as if the air has

altered somehow.' Mia shook her head, confused. 'Everything seems a little…wrong.' Then her face changed, twisting in sudden horror, and she darted off up the steep little beach, climbing to higher ground and then into an old and twisted tree that jutted out over the water. She stood on one of the branches, peering out between the leaves to the sea. 'The ships!' she whispered, so quietly that Ara and Lorin could scarcely hear her. 'The ships are here! They're inside the lagoon!'

'Will they have missed you?' Lorin murmured, as they swam back towards the palace. 'All those servants, will any of them have seen that you've been away all night?'

Mia wrapped her arms tight around Lorin's neck. 'I shouldn't think so. It's still early and they usually wait to be called. The girl who lights my bedroom fire might have noticed, I suppose.'

Lorin twisted round to look over her shoulder at Mia. 'Child, does no one watch over you at all?'

Mia shrugged. 'Not really. My ladies-in-waiting hate being assigned to me, you see. Because of who my mother was. They're glad when I don't need them and they can sit in the salons and gossip and complain about me.' She laughed sadly. 'If only they knew! They'd have so much more to gossip about. Oh, poor Ara! Do you think her sisters will listen? She looked so frightened.'

'Who knows…' Lorin murmured. 'They aren't creatures of the city, the way we horses are. They know only the sea. Ara is unusual among her kind, the way she tried to come into the city to chase down her little dream child. Mia, look there! Who is that girl, sitting on the jetty?'

The jetty ran around the edge of the pavilion outside the palace, so the duchess's gondola could draw up there, and she could alight to her favourite rooms of the palace. There was a gondola waiting there now, but out at the far end of the jetty was a girl in a white dress, rather grubby and tattered.

Mia leant forward over Lorin's ears and frowned.

'She must be one of the servants. She should be careful – if the chamberlain catches her like that, he'll turn her out at once.'

Lorin snorted, and flicked her ears. 'Are you sure she's a servant? There's a look about her, something familiar. She looks a little like you…'

Mia straightened up so suddenly that she nearly slid off Lorin's back, wide as it was. 'That's my cousin!' she hissed. 'Stop, Lorin. I don't want her to see me. Wait here, by these boats.'

'Your cousin?' Lorin sounded disbelieving. 'Your cousin's a duchess, Mia. That's a servant girl in a torn dress.'

'It is,' Mia muttered. 'I know her frock's all torn, but it *is* her. What on earth's she doing sitting there?'

Lorin peered furtively around the moored skiff, and sniffed. 'Crying.'

'Really?' Mia looked too. Her cousin *didn't* cry. Mia had never seen her look anything less than sweetly serene. 'Yes, you're right, she is…' Her voice trailed away doubtfully. She had hated Olivia with such a passion for so long that her cousin had become a strange sort of figure in her life – half real, and half imagined. She had been built up in Mia's head into a cruel, emotionless monster – even when the old Olivia, the smiling cousin who had first shown her the beauty of the water horses, threatened to topple the imaginary one.

Even the Olivia she thought back to now, the Olivia from before, didn't cry.

'Watch her tears,' Lorin murmured.

'What do you mean?' Mia squinted across the water. The sun was well up now, and the sea was dancing with little glittery ripples.

'Her magic is in her tears – watch when they fall in the water.'

'Ohhhh…' Mia sighed enviously as she saw what Lorin meant. Olivia was kneeling on the jetty, leaning out over the water, and her tears were dripping down her face and off her chin in a most undignified, unduchessy sort of way. But when the tears hit the water, they took her magic with them, spilling out great dancing pictures on the surface of the sea.

'Oh, I want to see them,' Mia whispered. 'I can't see what they are.'

'Water horses,' Lorin whispered, cutting silently through the water, creeping a little closer around the moored boats. 'And other creatures – I can't tell either. If only we could get closer without her seeing us!'

There was a tension between the two of them, a terrible eagerness to see those dancing images more closely. Perhaps even to swim amongst them, and dance with the creatures themselves.

'Do you think she knows what she's doing?' Mia breathed to Lorin. 'Those are her thoughts, aren't they? Her nightmares,' she added sadly, looking at her cousin's twisted shoulders, and the ends of her hair dangling in the water. She hadn't even noticed she was getting wet.

'Sometimes I forget how strong she is,' Lorin whispered. 'So much magic that it even leaks out in her tears.'

'I suppose we shouldn't watch,' Mia said. She felt ashamed to be spying, but she couldn't drag herself away from those dancing pictures. 'I'd hate it if she saw me crying…'

At that point the dancing figures swirled and disappeared in a pool of blackness and Olivia jumped up, staring angrily across the water.

'Who's there?' she cried.

Neither Mia nor Lorin thought of running, though they could easily have sneaked back through the moored boats and away out to the lagoon. Instead, with Lorin's head hanging, they moved through the water to Olivia.

Olivia's face lightened a little as she saw the water horse creeping towards her. But then she recognised the girl on Lorin's back. 'You!' she whispered, gazing wide-eyed at Mia.

Lorin drew up by the jetty, and Mia clambered off her back, made clumsy by a strange mixture of embarrassment and fear – and a small, growing knot of hope inside her.

'You said you didn't believe any more...' Olivia murmured. 'You said you couldn't see them.'

'I was lying.' Then Mia flinched at the expression on her cousin's face. *She thinks I'm like my mother.* 'It wasn't that way! I didn't want anything to do with magic, or the water horses, because I thought they were yours, and I hated you. It wasn't some horrible deceitful plot. Oh, don't you see? I was just angry!'

'So angry that she pretended to forget about me, Your Grace,' Lorin put in quietly. 'She cut herself off from all of us, and from her own magic. She buried it inside herself, and let it fester.'

'Lorin!' Mia looked at her in shock.

'It's true. I do not think your mother's spell would have grown so strong in you, Mia, if you had let your own magic grow too. That spell filled the place inside you where your magic should have been.'

'A spell?' Olivia demanded sharply.

Mia raised her eyes reluctantly to her cousin's face. 'Do you remember Mama's dresses? The way she always had an underskirt with golden embroidery? That heavy, raised embroidery in gilt thread – I used to love to stroke it.' She swallowed. 'She was using it to bind me.'

Olivia put out her hand and touched Mia's wrist, quite hesitantly, like an uncertain girl, as if she were not a duchess at all. 'She did the same to me.'

Mia nodded. 'But you broke all her spells, didn't you? I didn't! I promise that I didn't know!' Olivia subsided down onto the jetty again, and Mia knelt beside her, seizing her cousin's hands. 'I thought she loved me,' she whispered. 'I was so sure that no one else did – I'd convinced myself to forget even Lorin. I hung onto that golden thread that bound me to my mother. She poured her magic down it, and into me.' She felt her cousin's hands tense, as though she was about to pull them back. 'Please listen!' Mia begged. 'I've tried to tear it out of me, and some of it's gone. We got rid of it, me and— Me and Lorin,' she went on, after a second's pause. 'But she might still be able to make me do things.'

'Tell her.' Lorin whinnied sharply and pawed the water, striking up a great cloud of spray.

Mia hunched her shoulders, drawing herself into a miserable ball. Now her cousin would exile her too. 'I came to your room to hurt you. With a knife.'

Olivia laughed, which was so unexpected that Mia simply sat back and looked at her, with her mouth hanging open.

'Do you really think that you could walk into my room, Mia? In my palace, in my city, you could walk into my room and I wouldn't know that you were there?'

'You *knew*?' Mia whispered.

'And I watched you struggle.' She frowned. 'It was stupid of me not to see that you were under a spell – I simply thought that you could not bring yourself to kill me.'

'I never *wanted* to!' Mia wailed.

'The spell is the truth, Your Grace,' Lorin said. 'I saw her try to break its power. She was horrified by what she'd been made to do.'

'So was I,' Olivia pointed out sadly. 'I came out here to grieve for my pretty little yellow-haired cousin. Did you see yourself in my thoughts on the water?'

'No,' Mia whispered. 'I wasn't that close.'

'You were gone, I thought, and so many other beautiful creatures will be gone too, when the Talish turn Venice into another tiny outpost of the Empire.'

'Have you seen the ships?' Mia asked huskily, glancing back to look for them. The great galleys and warships sat hulking in the channel where the lagoon opened out into the wider sea.

'Yes. There are too many. I will have to give in and marry that idiot prince. Perhaps that way at least I can sweeten our defeat and gather up a few crumbs of favour from his father. Enough to beg for their mercy for my darling horses – and whatever else is out there in the water.'

'You can't!' Mia begged.

'What else can I do?' her cousin asked wearily. 'Would you rather we fought, and then they tore us all to bits, looking for every seed and grain of magic we have in us? We haven't a choice. A graceful surrender, that's all there is.' The tears began to slide slowly down her cheeks again, and Mia watched them, with a knot of misery deep inside. Her cousin's tears glittered brightly against her pale skin, and inside each one a tiny, silvery horse was dancing.

CHAPTER NINE

MIA REACHED OUT TO brush the tears away. She felt she couldn't bear to watch those dancing horses any longer. But as she stretched out her hand, a sudden sense of terror and dismay overtook her, leaving her gasping. She collapsed onto the jetty and wrapped her arms over her head, whimpering in panic.

'What is it? What's the matter?' Lorin demanded, rearing out of the water, her mane flying.

Olivia knelt down on the jetty, cradling Mia in

her arms. 'Is it your mother's spell?' She held her hand over Mia's heart, and began to murmur a spell of her own.

'It isn't,' Mia gasped out. 'Something's happened – Ara!'

'Who is Ara? What is she talking about?' Olivia pulled at Lorin's mane, but the water horse didn't answer. She was nuzzling anxiously at Mia.

'They're coming!' Mia whispered.

'Is it the ships?' Lorin let out a frightened whinny. 'Have the Talish monsters captured her?'

At that moment, a great fountain of water burst out of the sea close by the jetty, showering them all with spray. Mia sat up, staring, and Lorin hissed with disbelief.

A huge white water horse was turning and tumbling in the water beside them, twisting round and round as he fought to keep a grip on the creature he was fighting. She spat and clawed, thrashing her glinting red-golden tail, trying to slip out of his grasp like a fish. But he had a hank of her red hair clamped tightly in his teeth and he was dragging her, slowly but inexorably, towards the jetty and Olivia.

'A mermaid?' Olivia stood up, gaping at the frantic creature. 'Lucian, you've caught a mermaid?'

'Ara!' Mia screamed. 'Let her go, you're hurting her!'

'You *know* her?' Olivia demanded.

Lucian turned to look at Mia, and Ara took advantage of his distraction, clawing him across the muzzle with her nails and yanking her hair out of his mouth. Then she shot through the water to Mia.

'Tell me you're all right?' Mia begged. 'I could feel – he was dragging you—'

'Did you have to treat her so cruelly?' Lorin snapped, rounding on the larger horse, who backed away so shocked he looked almost foolish, with three oozing scratches tracked across his pinkish muzzle.

'She was skulking just out there, almost at the channel, by the ships! What was I supposed to do? I thought she was a Talish spy!' he snorted angrily.

'She's a mermaid!' Lorin reared up again in fury.

'Another creature of the water, just like us – you think she would work for the enemy?'

'Why not? Your precious child is!' Lucian snarled back. 'My lady's own little cousin. Or didn't she tell you that? Poor deluded Lorin, moping for years over a traitor's brat. And now a traitor yourself, but too foolish to see it!'

Lorin let out a high, eerie scream, and plunged at him, her dark hooves suddenly fearsome.

'Stop it! Stop!' Mia yelled, terrified by Lucian's huge teeth and his flailing, thrashing legs. He was so much bigger than Lorin. The silver mare looked tiny and delicate beside him, and even though she was fighting as viciously as she could, Mia was sure the larger horse would kill her in his fury. 'Lorin, come back! Please!'

'Mia, take my hand.' Olivia grabbed at her. 'They can't hear us, they're too angry. Lucian is terrified about the ships, and he can't bear that they're invading his water. He's taking it out on Lorin.'

'He'll kill her,' Mia sobbed.

'We won't let him. Hold my hand and join in my spell. I can feel your magic in you now – you can do this with me.'

Mia slipped her hand into Olivia's, and she felt the magic begin to build at once, circling around them like a whirlwind. Even in her fear for Lorin, there was a tiny moment of delight as the power skipped inside her and her own magic coiled around her cousin's, like two purring cats.

The two girls shivered as another magic joined theirs, an older, deeper magic. Mia pressed close against Olivia, frightened by the cold and the way it called to her.

'What is it?' she whispered. The power was theirs to call on – she could feel it – but she wasn't sure she dared.

'The sea,' Olivia said in a low, shocked voice. 'She's giving us the sea.' She nodded towards Ara.

The mergirl had climbed out onto the jetty. Even with her arms scratched and her hair torn and dishevelled, she was strong, and somehow more ancient than Mia had ever seen her look before. Her eyes were closed and her hands reached towards the water, drawing out the power of the unstoppable tides. 'Take it,' she murmured. 'I can't call it for long.'

'Step out onto the water,' Olivia told Mia. 'We have to stop this fight. Lorin is frantic, but this is too dangerous for her. She won't run from him, even when she should.'

Mia swallowed and stepped out from the jetty, expecting that they would have to swim to the fighting, thrashing horses. She hoped that her cousin was a better swimmer than she was. But as they walked out onto the sea, it held, giving very slightly under their feet, like the softest carpet.

Mia gripped Olivia's hand tightly and fought not to think how impossible this was – and how much water there was underneath them. As they approached the horses, the water churned under their feet and Mia tried not to panic as they stepped between the waves. She felt her cousin's hand tighten on hers as they came within reach of the flying hooves…and kept walking.

'Hold up your hand,' Olivia murmured, as they walked nearer, and Mia tried not flinch as Lorin's mane swirled past, a finger's width from her face. A faint shining of magic was all that showed they were protected.

'They can't hurt us?' she whispered to Olivia, trying to see the edges of the shielding spell.

'If they kicked us full on, with all their strength, they could. But I'm hoping they'll see us before that. The shield is only to protect us until they do.'

'So we have to walk in between them, and hope?'

Her cousin smiled. 'Do you trust me?'

No, Mia wanted to say, but then she remembered that dark moment in her cousin's room, fighting with the knife. Olivia had let her go free. 'Almost,' she whispered instead, and felt her cousin laugh.

They walked on, into the space of quiet air between the two fighting beasts, and Mia felt the passing breath of a hoof as it flailed by her cheek.

There was a horse's terrified scream, and then silence.

Then, 'Are you mad?' Lucian hissed furiously. 'Did you want us to kill you?'

'No.' Olivia smiled at him. 'We wanted you not to kill each other.'

'We wouldn't…we weren't…' he growled, his sides heaving. But then he glanced at Lorin, now slumped sideways in the water, her mane and tail swirling slackly in the tide. 'My sister! No!' He nosed at her frantically, lifting her lolling head with his own.

She coughed and pinkish foam spattered out of her nostrils. Mia began to weep – Lorin looked so broken. 'She was fighting for me,' she hissed at Lucian. 'If you've killed her, I will never forgive you, never.'

'I would not forgive myself,' the great horse said, gazing in horror at Lorin's feeble breathing. 'Little sister, wake up…I never meant…'

Mia shoved him aside, holding Lorin's great head in her arms and pressing her face against the glittering hair. Beside her, Ara stroked Lorin's muzzle and whispered to her – quiet, secret words. Was it her imagination, or was Lorin's dear mane already losing its brightness? 'Don't die,' Mia begged. 'You have to show him you were right, that we aren't traitors. If you die, *he wins*.'

Lorin coughed faintly, and one of her enormous dark eyes opened a little. 'I won…' she whispered.

'Yes, yes,' Mia told her lovingly. 'Of course you did. Even though he's bigger than you are.' She felt Lucian shift uncertainly beside her, and she glared at him.

'You are a sweet child,' Lorin whispered. 'Sweet of you to lie to me.' She struggled up a little and Mia saw trails of Ara's magic wafting from her nostrils. The mermaid swam back, eyeing the water horse, and Lorin swung her head dizzily and then pawed at the sea.

'You healed her?' Lucian stared at Ara.

'And I would not do the same for you.' Ara glared coldly at Lucian. 'Bring the two girls back to the palace. We need to talk, and their spell is weakening.'

'Yes.' The water horse nodded, humble for a moment. 'Ride on me, the two of you,' he murmured to Olivia, and Mia climbed astride him behind her cousin, her arms around Olivia's waist. Lorin followed, as they swam slowly back to the pavilion, and Mia turned back, watching her anxiously. But there were no visible wounds – the silver mare looked simply weary.

'Where have you come from, mermaid?' Lucian demanded, as they entered the shelter of the pavilion and Ara stretched herself gracefully across the gilded floor. Her tail fin stirred gently in the water and her rich golden scales made the gilt furniture look cheap and tawdry. 'Where have you come from, and what do you want?' he demanded again, shaking his mane furiously. 'If you are not a Talish spy, why have you appeared now, so suddenly? Why were you sneaking towards the palace?'

'I came to see Mia,' the mermaid said, glaring

proudly at the horse. 'The child you called a traitor. At least *she* has tried to raise the power of the sea against these Talish. You have all been doing nothing – nothing! – to halt the great black ships!'

Olivia laughed, a strange sobbing laugh. 'I suppose it seems like that to you,' she whispered.

'Mia warned me,' Ara went on. 'She wanted me to persuade my sisters and the other creatures of the deep sea to fight with you. She argued that if you lost these invaders would steal our magic, and use us for their own purposes.'

'Have they listened?' Mia asked eagerly. 'Do they understand now?'

Ara sighed. 'The water is dark with the shadows of the black ships. All of us can feel them lurking there, drawing the light out of our sea. And so we have come – I have come as their envoy – to tell you what we must do.'

Lucian's ears flickered angrily, but Olivia pressed her hand against his muzzle and he subsided, muttering.

'There is a way to destroy this fleet,' Ara went on slowly.

Olivia caught her breath. 'I can't trust that my magic is strong enough to defeat them – even with all the court magicians to help me build a spell. The Talish have magic of their own, a different power to ours, strong in metalwork and building, not so linked to their land. But even though it doesn't have the strength of a water magic, it's still clever and cunning. We could end up simply making everything worse. And I feel so for the men! This isn't the sailors' battle – they're caught up in it as much as we are. I already have a guard spell across the lagoon – that's why the ships are waiting just inside the channel. But it's taking half my strength to keep it up, and I can feel their mages pressing against it even now.'

'I am not talking about magic.' Ara looked at them all for a moment. 'This is a great secret. A deep secret. It is exactly what your Talish enemies have come here hoping to find. If we use this, it will be once, and once only. And then we will leave – we will go further and deeper, where we will be safe from human wars again.'

'You'll go?' Mia whispered, her eyes wide.

'We will. And so will most of the creatures of the deeper sea.' She glanced at Lorin and Lucian. 'Your horses, I expect, will stay.'

'This is our city,' Lucian snorted.

'And it is our sea! But we have been dragged into the city's battle,' Ara shot back. 'We cannot let this happen again, however hard it is for us – some of us – to leave.' She laid her hand on Mia's for a scant second, and then looked away.

'What is this way?' Olivia asked, frowning. 'How can we defeat the Talish without magic?'

'You must raise the Leviathan,' Ara told her simply.

Mia blinked, looking around at the others. She had never heard of the Leviathan, and had no idea what it was.

'There's no such thing,' Olivia said, but she sounded doubtful – as though that was what she had always been told, but now she wasn't quite sure.

'What is a Leviathan?' Mia whispered.

'Only a story.' Olivia nodded firmly, and Mia wondered if she were trying to convince herself too. 'A myth that sailors tell. It doesn't exist.'

'But you didn't think there were mermaids either,' Mia pointed out.

'I suspected there might be!' Olivia shot back. 'But the Leviathan isn't real. It can't be true.'

'Have you seen it?' Mia asked Ara.

The mermaid nodded. 'Yes. A great, reptilian creature. He lies sleeping on the sea bed, and he has slept for centuries. Occasionally he sighs, or his sleep is restless, and your waters rise or fall, or churn up in strange tides.'

'But if this is true…' Olivia murmured. 'The floods that wore out my father's magic. Were they caused by this creature?'

Ara nodded. 'Perhaps.'

Lucian snorted. 'I have never seen this thing.'

'And how would you?' Ara retorted. 'I told you, he's asleep. You would think his spine was a rocky outcrop on the sea bed. No one sees him.'

'What will happen if he wakes up?' Mia asked.

'He will rise up out of the water – and the Talish fleet will be beached upon his back.' Ara looked thoughtfully at Olivia, and added, 'If you wish to save the sailors, you could put rafts in the water, maybe.'

'He wouldn't be angry? At being woken?' Lorin asked, a little nervously.

Ara took a while to answer, and at last she shrugged and said again, 'Perhaps. But my sisters have sometimes told stories of his waking, just for a moment. He twitches, and a great eye opens, and he looks around him, as if to see whether anything has changed. And then he goes back to sleep. He's cold-blooded, and slow – not quick to anger, like the rest of us. But I think he would be angry, if we told him the danger we were in. He would be glad to ground the fleet.'

A great dark, glinting eye. Mia shivered. She had seen that in her dreams. Had she met this Leviathan already? She glanced around, and saw that Olivia was watching her.

'You've seen this creature before, haven't you?' Olivia whispered.

Mia looked back into her cousin's eyes. Even at sixteen, Olivia was scarcely taller than she was. 'How did you know?'

'Something in your face. Are you frightened?'

'Yes… But not of him, exactly. He seemed kind, I think…'

Ara took both Mia's hands, searching her face. 'You had better come with me, then. If you've seen him before, in your dreams, you may be able to help us wake him.'

'You can't take her,' Olivia protested. 'She's too young. It isn't safe.'

Lorin nudged the duchess gently. 'My lady, no one is safe. Not now.'

Lucian snorted, shaking his mane and pawing at the water. He wanted to be out there, fighting, Mia could tell. Just like she did.

'I want to help,' she pleaded, and at last Olivia sighed, and nodded to the mermaid. 'Who knows what will happen if we wake this creature. But if it works... It seems to be our only choice. Though I fear what will happen to the city when it rises up and disturbs the sea bed so completely. We shall have to weather a flood greater than any we have had in years, I suspect.'

Lucian shook his mane angrily, as though he wanted to argue again. But all he said was, 'So, how do we wake up this sleeping beast?'

CHAPTER TEN

'DO YOU KNOW HOW to do this?' Mia whispered to Ara, once Olivia had hurried back through the private passageway between the water chamber and her staterooms. She had to change out of her bedraggled petticoat before she summoned her councillors to discuss the raising of the Leviathan, and the protection of the city from the expected floods. Lucian had gone out into the canals to call in the other water horses.

Ara looked thoughtfully out at the ships.

They were close enough that Mia was sure she could see men moving about on the decks. There seemed so many of them, busying about like little ants. Mia shivered, as she imagined the ships suddenly rising out of the water on the back of the great beast under the sea, and all those tiny bodies falling. She hated and feared the Talish, but she was glad that her cousin wanted to rescue the sailors. *And Mama and Zuan*, a small voice whispered inside her head. Although surely her mother's magic would save them?

Ara stirred her tail in the greenish water, and sighed. 'No. No one has ever done it.'

Mia sat down next to her, dipping her feet in the water. 'So – maybe he can't even be woken.'

Lorin made an irritated noise, as if she was sucking her teeth. 'She told you that he opens his eyes, Mia. Have a little faith.'

'I'm sorry,' Mia said wearily. 'Everything keeps changing. Three days ago, I didn't have magic, I'd only dreamed of mermaids, and I didn't speak to my cousin unless I was forced to. And now this…' She couldn't help thinking of that dark eye she had seen in her dreams. It had never scared her, then – but it had only been a dream. Now she knew that it was real, and the thought of the creature that went along with that eye was making her stomach clench with fear. She wasn't sure she could even imagine anything so huge. She leant against Lorin's silvery side and let out a shaky, frightened breath.

Lorin nuzzled her ear. 'Aren't things better this way?' she asked, her voice a low rumble. There was a note of pleading in there too, and Mia stretched her arm as far as it would go around her neck, hugging tight.

'You know it is,' she whispered. 'I have you again. And we broke my mother's spell, so I can stay here safely. Now the Talish will go…' She faltered a little, remembering what Ara had said.

'Why do *you* have to leave?' Lorin asked, peering round at Ara, her dark eyes sad.

Ara hunched her shoulders a little. 'We don't speak to humans. We stay down deep in the sea, and when we come out of the water, we hide ourselves. That's the way it's always been, to keep ourselves safe. Humans are – greedy. And jealous, and fascinated. We stay away. That's the way it's always been,' she repeated sadly.

Mia wanted to argue, to say that humans weren't like that at all, that *she* wasn't like that. That Olivia and the city would treat the mermaids with love, and even awe. But she suspected that Ara was right. After all, the Talish had proved the mermaids' point. The water creatures were only leaving because it was no longer safe to stay.

Mia caught her breath as she saw her cousin coming down the marble steps. Olivia was making as grand an entrance as she could, preceded by pages piping on tiny golden flutes, and with the members of her council parading behind her, followed by a curious mass of courtiers. The young duchess was wearing a black velvet dress that made Mia wince, it looked so heavy. The underskirt was silver lace, scattered with fat pink pearls, and it had a shoulder train, which trailed down the steps after Olivia with a silken whisper.

Mia was sure that it was one of the grandest dresses that her cousin owned. Olivia was using her wardrobe as a weapon – the black dress was not to be argued with.

Unfortunately, the beauty of the black dress only made Mia's damp and filthy night robe look even worse. She felt Lorin moving closer as the court approached, shielding her with the glittering fall of her mane. But then a small page boy darted out from behind her cousin, making for Mia and Lorin, where they stood by the opening to the pavilion. He held a cushion, on which lay a folded pile of clothes.

'Her Grace says you're to go in there and change, my lady.' He nodded to the door to Olivia's private rooms. 'Just in there. Her Grace says these will be suitable for riding in.'

Mia took the clothes and darted into the little anteroom behind the door. It was a relief to get rid of the nightgown, but the new clothes were equally odd. Her cousin had sent her a boy's tunic and woollen leggings – in fact, Mia would not have been surprised if they were part of the livery of the very boy who had handed them to her. Could she wear these? What would all those gossipy ladies-in-waiting say?

Mia clicked her tongue in disgust. She didn't care! Or at least, she did care, but she knew that it was stupid of her. She had to ride Lorin out to the sea past Sant'Erasmo – and there, she and Ara were to raise a centuries-old beast from the bottom of the sea. Fifteen- and sixteen-year-old ladies-in-waiting sniggering at her behind their hands was the least of her worries. She smoothed the tunic down over her front, resting her hands lightly on her ribs, where that sense of joyous magic had grown, and tried to look as though she wasn't scared.

There was an eerie hush as she stepped out of the anteroom. Mia stopped for a moment, looking around her and wondering what had gone wrong. But it was only that everyone was watching her, and waiting –

almost as if they expected her to be different.

I am different, Mia told herself grimly. *I won't be just a traitor's daughter any more. If this works, they will have to stop whispering. Or at least, they can whisper about something I actually* did.

Olivia held out her hand and Mia took it, standing next to her cousin and hearing the little hissing words go running around the chamber. She reached out her other hand and wrapped it tightly in Lorin's mane, for comfort.

'Don't listen,' Olivia whispered, kissing her on the forehead and patting her cheek. 'And remember that I trust you, even after that night in my rooms. Be careful. Oh, Mia, you're shaking…'

'I'm just scared of the bigness of everything. It matters, so much. I'm not used to mattering,' Mia added huskily. 'No one notices what I do.'

'Lorin always watched over you.' Olivia caressed the silver mare's soft nose. 'So did I. Even when all you did was scowl at me, and you talked as if any words you had to speak to me were poisonous.'

Mia frowned, staring at her feet. 'Why didn't you ever tell me yourself what my mother had done?'

Olivia sighed. 'I always meant to. But you were so little, and so happy. Then suddenly all that changed, and I realised I was too late. You were horribly angry, and whenever I tried, after that, I could see that you weren't hearing me – you heard what you thought I was saying, and that was all. I don't know how much of that was you, and how much was your mother's spell, twisting your thoughts.'

'I don't know either,' Mia admitted. 'I don't feel that way now. And I always loved the city. I couldn't bear the thought of leaving, even when I wanted so much to be with my mother and brother.' She kissed Olivia back. 'I'd better go. Ara's waiting, out there in the water past the jetty. We don't know how long it will take.'

Olivia nodded, and her smile drooped for a second.

Mia threw her arms around her cousin tightly, ignoring the horrified gasp from half the court, and the little voice inside her that said one did not hug duchesses. Olivia had looked so tired and frightened, just in that second.

Olivia hugged her back, smiling again. 'Try not to be too long,' she whispered in Mia's ear, and Mia thought that she was trying not to look behind her at the councillors and the courtiers, all eager to catch their words. 'They're pushing so hard against the shield we can't hold it for much longer. Jac and the others have hardly slept in days, and we're weakening…'

Mia nodded, then walked out to the jetty, Lorin pacing proudly beside her. She could feel the courtiers pressing and jostling – most politely – behind them. Although the plan had not been made public, in case word got out to the Talish and the ships were moved, everyone knew that something was about to happen. And that the duchess's strange little bad-blood cousin was mixed up in it all.

A moment after they stepped out onto the jetty, Mia felt the sudden lift of tension and excitement in the air around them. She had expected that Ara would meet them further out in the water, that she would be concealed beside one of the boats or hidden by her magic, if she was in the open water. Instead, the mermaid was still sitting at the end of the wooden platform – her hair combed out and flowing over her shoulders in long red waves.

Mia ran along the jetty, forgetting to be dignified. 'What are you doing?' she demanded crossly. 'You should be hiding – they can all see you!'

'I know.' Ara smiled sweetly at her and took her hand. 'That's why I'm here. So that all those stupid girls see me, and know that it was you who found us.'

'But I thought it had to be a secret.'

'Oh, Mia. It did. It was the deepest secret.' Ara slipped into the water, her scales flashing in the sunlight. 'But tomorrow we'll be gone. It won't matter who knows. Except that they will always remember you as the girl who knew the mermaids.'

Lorin leapt out into the water, and circled round for Mia to climb onto her back.

'You really are going, then,' Mia said, as Ara drew

in beside the water horse.

Ara didn't answer – she simply stretched out her arms and began to swim towards the ships.

Out in the lagoon, just beyond the great islands of Sant'Erasmo and Le Vignole, the black ships gathered in a hulking mass. They made Mia think of crows, circling round some poor sick animal, waiting for it to give in and die.

She was seized with a sudden fit of trembling, as she saw the crow-ships tearing her city apart. She had never had premonitions – it was only that she was scared. It was not *true*.

'We're here.' Ara surfaced again and swam back towards Mia and Lorin, waiting in the channel between the islands. Ara looked paler than ever – she was frightened too. Mia tried to think of the gentle, curious feeling she'd had from that watching eye, not the size of the rest of the Leviathan.

'It's under us then?' Lorin asked, squinting a little to see down into the water. She was not a deep-sea creature – the water horses spent all their time in the water, or at least touching it, but they did not often submerge themselves completely. Still, if Mia hadn't been on her back, she would have followed Ara down to the sea floor.

'I wish I could come with you under the water,' Mia sighed, thinking of the cool, dim world of her dreams.

Lorin snorted. 'If he's as big as she says he is, we'll see him soon enough. Come on. Those ships are making me feel strange – they seem to be getting larger every time I look at them.'

Mia shuddered. 'I think it's a spell – they were giving me strange visions too. They've set a spell around them, to make them look even more fearsome than they really are.'

Ara laughed. 'Good. Then perhaps they don't realise how scared everyone in the city is already. I've found the ridge of spikes along the Leviathan's spine. And over there, back towards that island' – she pointed over at Le Vignole – 'there's an underwater hill. I think that's his head.'

Mia swallowed, and nodded, and Lorin swam after Ara towards the island. Lorin waded through the clear, shallow water until she was chest-deep, then turned to stand looking back at the sea, so calm and blue. Ara floated next to them, holding Lorin's mane.

'We need to join our magic together,' she said. 'It's easiest if we have something to hold – like when we held the black stone. Mia, can you pluck out one of your hairs? We'll all do it – to help us weave our magic together.'

Mia twisted her damp fair hair around one finger and pulled out a single hair. Ara handed her a long, red strand, much thicker than her own, and Lorin snorted. 'You'd better pull one out for me, I can't.'

Mia set her teeth and whipped a hair out of Lorin's mane.

Ara nodded. 'Now plait them together.' Mia began to twist the strands – silver, golden and red – while Ara watched. After Mia had completed a finger's length of plaiting, the mergirl added, quite matter-of-factly, 'Now say the spell.'

'What spell?' Mia gaped at her.

'Don't stop plaiting! And I don't know, Mia, but this is your city, so it needs to be you that draws our magic together and wakes him.'

Mia plaited on, slowly, stroking the threads together and trying to think. If only Ara had warned her. Perhaps it was better as a surprise. If she'd known she'd have to say a spell, she would have worried over it so much she'd never get it right. She could feel the strength of each thread of hair in her fingers now. The strength of the ocean currents and the slow green depths of the canals built inside her, aching inside her fingers, so that she was desperate to send the spell down into the water.

'Thread of the dark sea, thread from the light,' she murmured to her plaiting fingers. 'Thread from the city, together we fight. *Oh!*' The hairs were glowing, and sealing together into one pinkish-shining braid. Mia could feel her magic, new and glorious, stirring inside her and reaching out to the braid, and the sea, and what was under the sea. The water around Lorin and Ara began to shimmer, and tiny jewel-like bubbles foamed around them.

A rich love of the tides, and the sandy depths of the sea, the sunny stretches and dark corners of the canals, surged through Mia as their magic joined. Deep down under the waters, she felt something stir, touched by the strange mixture of magic bubbling in the water above him. 'Take it!' she gasped. 'Take it down there and give it to him, Ara, *now*!'

Ara seized the braid and darted down into the water, disappearing in a flicker of amber-golden tail.

Seized by the magic, Mia slipped from Lorin's back and tried to follow the mermaid. She knew she shouldn't – that she wouldn't last down there in the dark, deep water, but she hadn't a choice. The magic was calling, and Ara had gone. Mia had to follow her – they were joined together in the spell, even as the coldness of the deeper waters sucked at the life inside her.

Please help us! she begged, trying to use the delicious magic inside her to show the ancient creature the beauties of her city – the canals, the horses, the statues and shrines on every little turn and corner of a *calle*, strings of washing stretched across a sunny waterway. And then the great dark ships, coming to steal away the beauty and the glory from the waters of Venice.

The cold-blooded, slow creature under the water warmed a little, fired by her glittering pictures, and she felt him stir a fraction more.

Make them go away – please...

The water was green and clear and icy cold, but already there was a mistiness spreading up from the sea floor, as the sand of centuries boiled and churned. Mia fought her way down, her lungs burning and her eyes stinging from the salt, aware of the great pale shape beside her that was Lorin, drawn down by the magic as she was.

Mia's breath was failing now, streams of crystal bubbles stealing away her precious air, and her magic had trailed away to a thread. But she fought on –

desperate to bring the great, ancient creature to the surface.

Black velvet darkness was starting to spread from the corners of Mia's eyes when she felt something catch her wrist and begin to drag her up again into the air.

'What were you thinking?' the mermaid screamed, as they broke the surface and she hauled Mia towards the shallows. 'Breathe!'

Mia coughed, chest burning. 'Where's Lorin?' she wheezed.

'Here.' Lorin dragged herself exhaustedly up onto the sand, standing fetlock-deep among the wavelets, head hanging. 'Mia, what was that spell? I've never felt anything so strong.' She brushed her mane affectionately against the mergirl's shoulder. 'You can't blame us for following you, Ara. I had to – it was unstoppable.'

'Did it work?' Mia coughed again, spitting out dribbles of seawater. 'Did he wake? I saw sand stirring, that was all, and then you pulled me away.'

But Ara wasn't listening. Her eyes had widened, and Mia turned to see where she was staring.

It was as if an island grew, a hundred ship-lengths out, between the larger islands that formed the mouth of the lagoon. The creature was so large that it was almost impossible to see him as a living being. Instead, he was the earth, moving, changing. As if the two islands were joining themselves together.

The head broke the surface first, rounded, blunt-nosed and lizard-like, the black eyes, the size of Mia herself, mild and amused.

'It worked…' Lorin shook her mane in surprise. 'Did he understand? Will he beach the ships? Shouldn't he be over there?' She pawed anxiously at the water with one hoof. 'Ara! He's in the wrong place!'

Mia laid her hand on Lorin's flank. 'No, he isn't, look. He's just – so big. Look! His back *is* under the ships. Oh no…'

It was too hard to watch. The fleet, which had seemed so menacing, suddenly looked like toys tossing on a pond kicked up by a child's tantrum. Mia had treasured a little ship like that, built for her by her cousin's shipwrights, made to sail along the canals on a golden string. For a confused, terrified moment, as the Leviathan's great head rose fully from the water and turned back to survey the tiny ships spilling away down his back, Mia wondered what had happened to her pretty toy. There was a terrifying moment of stillness as the ships stood silhouetted against the blueness of the sky. And then the great ships rose higher out of the water, and toppled and split apart, crashing down to the sea in a jumble of broken timbers. Mia hid her face in Lorin's soft coat, weeping.

'The rafts,' Lorin muttered. 'Where are the rafts your cousin promised?'

Mia looked up, blinking away tears. The sea was a boiling mass of debris, scattered with the bobbing heads of the sailors. The Leviathan himself was turning now, slowly, laboriously. He was making his way out through the channel, into the open sea beyond the lagoon.

'There!' Mia gasped in relief. A few of the broken timbers shifted in the water and formed a clumsy raft, next to a knot of struggling men, and then another appeared, and another. Each of the rafts was immediately swamped with sailors, climbing on and hauling each other aboard. As they filled up, the rafts began to move slowly but surely back towards Le Vignole, where Mia and the others were waiting, standing ankle-deep on a bank of sand.

'We should move,' Lorin murmured. 'We don't want to be here when they arrive. Why is she sending them here, and not back to the city?'

'This is the garrison island,' Mia explained. 'See? Over there, this island joins onto the fort on Sant'Andrea. The soldiers are already waiting.' She pointed over at the fort, now bristling with armed men. 'Olivia doesn't want the Talish sailors in the city itself. But yes, we should move.'

She looked back at the sailors – more rafts were appearing, and there were only a few heads left bobbing in the water now. She kept searching for her mother and Zuan – but how would she recognise them? At this distance, any of those water-sleeked heads could be her mother's, or her brother's. She doubted that they would be in the sea anyway – she was almost certain that Lady Sofia would have used magic to take them far away – but she still couldn't help looking.

'We shouldn't be here,' Ara said slowly. 'Mia, come here, hold tight to me. And to Lorin. Hold onto us.'

'Why? What is it?' Mia glanced between Ara and Lorin. Ara's face had paled, and her lips were drawn away from her sharp teeth in an eerie grin of fright. Lorin had laid her ears back, and she let out a panicked whinny.

'What is it?' Mia yelled, turning round to look where they were looking. What had she missed? Was the Leviathan coming back? Was he going to attack them?

She stared out to sea, and her stomach seemed to drop inside her. Where the Leviathan had risen, disrupting the centuries-old layers of the sea bed, a great disturbance had taken place. The waters were gathering in a seething mass, pulling back into the channel and gathering up the debris from the broken ships. The water dragged back, coiling the jetsam underneath itself as it surged up into a mighty wave. The sea sucked and hissed and boiled into a mass of dark water, tipped with creamy foam.

The water hung there, poised, for what seemed an impossible length of time – and then the wave broke, and ran roaring for the city.

CHAPTER ELEVEN

'I T'S GOING TO HIT THE city,' Mia screamed. She could hear panicked voices behind her as the soldiers watched the wave surging towards them.

'Where will it strike?' Lorin muttered, rearing up and then dropping back to paw at the damp sand around her feet. The water she had been standing in had been sucked out to feed the wave. 'Why didn't we think of this?' she demanded angrily. 'I have to get back to the city – we need to hold back the tide.'

'I don't think even the water horses can hold this

back,' Mia whispered. 'Oh, Lorin, I'm so sorry. We wanted to save the city, and we've only made everything worse.'

'No.' Lorin rested her muzzle against Mia's shoulder. 'No, never think that. Broken is better than enslaved, Mia. But I cannot let this happen without joining my brothers and sisters.'

'I don't think the main strength of the wave will hit the city,' Ara said suddenly. 'It's got to come past us first.'

Mia swallowed, watching the great mass of dark water. It was beautiful, in an awful way – the wave was translucent, like the best glass. 'Will it hit us?' she whispered, clutching tightly to Lorin's mane. 'Could we ride it out? At least – at least if it hits here, the city won't be destroyed.'

Ara frowned, twitching her tail in the water, almost as though she was trying to sense what it was doing. Perhaps she could, Mia realised. This was Ara's world, moving around her. 'No. Look – that smaller island where you said the fort was. Sant'Andrea. It will hit there first, it has to. Look at the way it's travelling. And then it will go on to strike that little island that sticks out to the east of the main city.'

'Sant'Elena,' Mia murmured, gazing at the wall of water. 'You're right. It's going to hit Sant'Elena. The church, and the monastery.'

'It will swamp the rest of the city too,' Ara said sadly. 'But not with such force. The main damage will be to the fort on Sant'Andrea, I think. Where it hits first.'

'What about the soldiers? And all the sailors that came in on the rafts? Olivia saved them for nothing!' Mia began to run stumbling along the damp sand, towards the channel that divided them from the tiny island of Sant'Andrea. She was screaming, begging the soldiers to run – but they were already disappearing, hauling the shipwrecked sailors with them back into the fort. The wave was so horrific they clearly could not bear to abandon their enemy to the water.

Mia stumbled on up the beach. 'They haven't got

time to get off the island,' she gasped. 'Can't we rescue them somehow?'

'Not all of them…' Lorin murmured, cantering round in front of Mia to head her off. Mia tried to dodge round the water horse, but Lorin caught her, grabbing the sleeve of Mia's tunic in her teeth.

'We have to help them!' Mia sobbed. 'Look at it!'

'Mia, stop! They're barricading themselves inside. It's a fort! It's built to withstand a broadside attack from the sea. They have more chance staying put. Even if we tried to get them all back on those rafts, or in their boats, they'd likely be caught in the wave. Their only chance is to stay behind those stone walls. The fort is built on the high ground – it's the shore that will take the worst of it.'

'She's right,' Ara called. 'We have to get you to safety somehow, Mia. Lorin and I might be able to survive this, but if it hits us, it will still be almost at its full strength. We have to get you away.'

'Where to?' Mia screamed above the roaring of the wave. It seemed to be moving faster and the water was hanging above them now, the white spray reaching down to her like claws. 'It's too late. There's no time!' She looked around, wondering if she could climb a tree – but that would mean leaving Lorin and Ara behind. Besides, the height of a tree could hardly make any difference.

'We have to go into the water. Mia, climb on me.' Lorin stood at the edge of the sea, the force of the oncoming wave sending her mane and tail flying back. 'I promise I will do the best I can to keep you safe. But we can't be here when the wave hits the land. We need to go out to sea.'

'Into the wave?' Mia mouthed at Lorin. The noise of the wave was too loud even for her to shout now.

Lorin nodded and Ara began to fight her way out across the thin skin of water that was all there was left of the sea, clawing with her hands, digging her tail into the sand.

'Put your arms around my neck!' Lorin screamed, kneeling down on her forelegs so Ara could reach. 'I'll pull you out there!'

With Ara and Mia hanging onto her mane, Lorin cantered heavily into the dead space below the oncoming wave. It towered over them like a wall of ink-blue glass, strangely still now that it was so close.

'Mia, take this.' Ara reached for Mia's hand, pressing a tiny silver bubble into her palm.

'What is it?' Mia tried to hold onto it, but it seemed to sink through her fingers.

'Swallow it,' Ara cried, trying to push Mia's hand towards her lips. 'It's air, Mia – we're going to hit the side of the wave, and you won't be able to breathe. You need it.'

As the water curled over them, Mia pressed the ball of air against her mouth, coughing at the sudden burning energy that filled her lungs – and then the wave hit, and she turned over and over in the water, carried away into darkness.

'She's dead.'

'She isn't, she's breathing.'

Mia could hear the voices – children, it sounded

like. She wondered who they were arguing about, who it was that might be dead. And then she slowly realised that it was herself.

'Not – dead,' she coughed out.

'Told you,' said the girl's voice, rather smugly.

Mia forced her eyes open – they were stuck and crusted with salt – and looked up at the two children, both a little younger than she was.

'Why are you wearing boys' clothes?' the girl asked her disapprovingly. 'You look ridiculous.'

Mia blinked around her, looking for Lorin and Ara and trying to work out where she was. It looked as though she had been carried into the city on the flood tide.

'Have you seen…?' She coughed up more water, turning and spitting it between the tangled mass of weed and timbers that she was lying on. She heard the prim little girl sniff disgustedly. 'Have you seen a water horse? Or a…?' She faltered to a stop. She couldn't even ask about Ara. Instead she blinked again, staring up at the great mass of whiteness above her. She had thought at first that she'd hit her head and she wasn't seeing properly, but now she gave a little sighing laugh. The dream-like white marble building was Santa Maria della Salute, the great church that one of her great-something-grandfathers had had built, as a thanksgiving after the city had survived a particularly evil bout of the plague. She had been swept right into the city, landing on the far bank of the mouth of the Grand Canal. If she could only sit up, she would be able to see the palace across the water.

'Ugh, what's that?' the fussy little girl cried out, and Mia decided dreamily that she really didn't like this child very much. 'Ugh, a giant slimy *fish*! Come on, Pietro! Let's go and look at that boat.' There was splashing, and the tumble of weeds shifted a little, as the two children hurried away.

Mia closed her eyes again, enjoying the sun on her face.

'Mia! Mia!'

Mia blinked, and wriggled sideways a little to see

who was speaking. Then everything the little girl had said settled properly in her head, and she sat up. 'Ara, are you under there?'

The clump of weed stirred faintly and Mia saw what the children must have seen – a tail fin, caught up in the debris. 'Can you move? Are you hurt?' she gasped, trying to creep across the shifting mass to reach the mermaid.

'I'm stuck. And Lorin is under here too – I can feel that I'm still holding her mane.'

Mia yanked at a piece of wood, hissing as she tore her fingertips on the sharp splinters – but she could see Ara's face now, pale, except for a dark bruise stretching up her cheek. The mermaid pushed weakly at the timber above her, and then dragged her tail out from the jumbled mess. 'Call Lorin,' she told Mia urgently. 'She'll listen to you. I can feel her trying to move, but I can't get at her. She keeps trying to kick out, and I think she's only dragging herself down further.'

'Lady Mia.'

The voice that spoke behind them was so like Lorin's that Mia turned in surprise, wondering if the water horse had somehow escaped without them seeing. But the horse in the water was larger than Lorin, a richly dappled grey with a mane that shone like polished iron.

'Lady Mia, if you climb back onto the steps, we can free our sister. She is too deeply entangled for you to lift the timbers. Can the gracious lady of the sea reach the water?'

Mia blinked at him, and realised that he must mean Ara. Many of the water horses did not often speak to the people of the city, and their speech was stuck several hundred years before. But Ara *was* a gracious lady of the sea, Mia thought, wrapping her arms around the mermaid and half rolling her towards the open water. Ara's tail was dusty and dry, and she sighed with delight as she slipped towards the cool water again. Mia jumped and clambered and wobbled back to the marble steps and sat down, with Ara leaning her arms wearily on the step beside her.

'You saved me,' Mia said, remembering the bubble of air and the crashing, thundering confusion as the wave had hit. 'I'd have drowned if you hadn't made us go out into the water.' She dragged lank streaks of hair out of her eyes and stared anxiously at the grey water horse who had spoken to her, and his two golden companions, busily tearing and kicking at the mat of debris.

'Look!' Ara caught her shoulder. 'What's he doing? Have they got her?'

A silver-white horse was struggling out of the debris, half supported by the darker grey, who had swum underneath to push her out.

'Lorin!' Mia started to run out to her, but then stood hesitating at the edge, frightened that she would send Lorin crashing through the timbers again if she pushed them off balance. But Lorin snorted and shook her mane, laying her ears back and snapping ungratefully at the dappled grey. She launched herself into the water and swam to Mia and Ara, nosing at them frantically.

The grey water horse snorted a laugh at his sister. 'Lorin, you fuss over them as if they're your own foals.'

Mia smiled at the grey over Lorin's head, which was cradled in her lap. She didn't think that Lorin even heard him.

'She swam with us into the wave,' Ara told the grey, gazing back at him proudly. 'We raised the creature off the sea bed, and set it to destroy the fleet. We swam the wave together and survived, all three of us. We aren't her foals. These are my sisters.'

'My lady.' The grey bowed his head again, and then looked up. 'Ladies, all of you, you should hasten back to the palace. Her Grace...has need of her little cousin.'

His voice had dropped, and Mia sat up, gazing at him anxiously. 'Why? What is it? Is Olivia hurt? Did the flood hit the palace so badly?'

The water horse didn't answer. Instead he swam out into the channel, looking back over his shoulder, clearly asking them to follow him.

The dappled grey escorted them back to the palace, nudging Lorin every so often when she foundered in the water. He tried to make her give Mia to him to carry, but Lorin shrieked at him and kicked out with her front hooves, so he contented himself with swimming as close beside her as he could. When they landed at the pavilion, he left to join the other water horses who were almost all still out in the canals. They were trying to help draw back the tide, and ferrying those who had been trapped in their houses by the floodwaters.

The storm surge had mostly died away, but there were pockets of flooding left here and there throughout the city. A few small children, those who were not too old to think they were seeing things, watched delightedly as Ara and the other mermaids helped by drawing the water down from their doors and sending it washing back towards the lagoon. Their glittering tails flashed in the murky waters of the canals, and the mermaids stared curiously in at the open windows, spying on the city.

Mia and Lorin stumbled wearily into the water chamber, where Mia found her cousin, looking more dead than alive.

'What happened to her?' Mia whispered, her voice choked with tears.

'The water,' Lucian murmured. 'The same thing that happened to her father. She tried to fight the water – she couldn't bear to see the flood surging over the city, and she tried to turn it back.'

Mia leant over her cousin, trying not to let her tears fall on Olivia's face. The duchess was lying on a gilded couch in the water chamber, guarded by her pages, and by Lucian. The black velvet dress showed up the greenish pallor of her skin. She seemed hardly even to breathe.

'Why doesn't she wake up?' Mia asked, stroking Olivia's face, hoping to see her smile and open her eyes.

'She's exhausted – she has drained her magic,' Lucian told her wearily, and Mia realised that he must have given most of his own power to Olivia as well. 'She turned back the force of the water as it came over Sant'Elena. And then she collapsed.'

'But – she will wake up?' Mia asked him, half sitting, half falling against her cousin's couch.

'I don't know.' Lucian stalked away from her, his tail switching from side to side.

'My lady.'

Mia looked up to find Signor Jac standing beside her.

'I must congratulate you. Her Grace and I worked a scrying spell on the water to watch your raising of the Leviathan. We felt the power of the spell, linking your magic with Lorin and the mermaid.' His dark eyes fixed on hers, full of wonder and a sort of terrified excitement.

Mia had always found the magician so frightening, but now she stared back at him and tried to smile.

'It was incredible.'

'I know,' Mia whispered. She looked out at the water, through the opening to the pavilion. 'You know they're going. We'll never see them again.

The mermaids are going to lead the Leviathan out to the deeper sea and hide him. Whatever else is out there in the water – all the things we've never even seen! They'll go too.' She twisted a lock of Lorin's mane between her fingers, and the silver horse sighed in her ear.

'I suppose they must.' Signor Jac rubbed his hand across his face, and sighed. 'If they stay here, they'd be in too much danger. You know the Talish will come back,' he added, glancing at Mia. 'Maybe not for another who-knows-how-many years. But this isn't over. And can't you just imagine what a shipbuilder, or a designer of war-machines, would do with that great creature? How many men they would have it carry? Think of it, Mia…' He traced one hand in front of her eyes, and suddenly there it was, the Leviathan, lunging heavily through the air. It swam almost as swiftly as it had before, but its eyes were dull, and its skin was metal-armoured, bristling with guns and bayonets.

'No…' Mia hissed.

'They'd enslave him, and all the other creatures of the deep water. It's safer for them to go. It would happen.'

Mia stood up and walked out to the pavilion, with Signor Jac and Lorin following her. 'I know it would. I know they have to leave. But it's only been such a short time. I don't *know* them!' she protested angrily. She knelt down on the jetty and watched the waves, lapping gently against the boats. The sun sent shadows glimmering and shifting on the water, sapphire and purple and green – and they were there.

Ara, and her sisters, watching her from between the wavelets. Smiling.

'Don't go…' Mia whispered pleadingly to Ara. And then she pressed her hand across her mouth, because she knew they had to.

The sun glittered over the sea again, and the mermaids were gone.

'No!'

Mia turned round, half blinded by tears, and saw her cousin, standing in the doorway. She had one arm around Lucian's neck, and it was clear that he was holding her up.

'You let them go?' Olivia stepped shakily out onto the jetty. 'How could you?'

'I had to!' Mia wept. 'Do you think I wanted to? It isn't safe for them to be here.'

'I know, I know.' Olivia rested her face against Lucian's neck for a moment. 'But so soon...'

'We could go after them,' Lorin said suddenly, looking up at Mia from the water. 'We could swim out, and say goodbye properly. Out in the sea, where they belong.'

Mia hesitated. She wanted so desperately to speak to Ara one last time. But what if they swam out through the channel and the mermaids were already gone? It would be heart-breaking.

'Go.' Olivia nodded to her. 'Otherwise you'll always wish you had.'

Mia flung herself onto Lorin's back and they set off, gliding through the water, avoiding the broken timbers and knots of weed that dotted the lagoon.

They swam in silence as they passed Sant'Andrea and the fort, its stone walls still solid, even though the stands of trees along the coastline had been tumbled and torn.

They passed into the channel between the Lido and the mainland, and Lorin hissed at the jumble of spars and tangled ropes littered across the water.

'There were so many ships,' Mia whispered. 'I wonder which one my mother was on... What's that?' She sat up, staring in horror, and then let out a shaky laugh as a painted figurehead rolled sickeningly past them. For a moment, in the dip between two waves, she had thought it was a woman, golden-haired and dreadfully still.

Lorin huffed a little through her nostrils. 'Mia, she never came for you. She never wrote, or begged your cousin to let you have her back. Forget her.'

'I know.' Mia leant forward, wrapping her arms tightly around Lorin's neck. 'Ara called us her sisters, did you hear her? I know she's gone, but I'll always remember that. I have you, and I have Olivia, and I have the mermaids in my thoughts, for ever.' She wound a lock of Lorin's mane around her wrist, feeling its warmth, the loving strength in all the hairs. 'I don't need my mother…'

It was as she spoke the word, soft and murmuring, that the spell set upon her. The last remnants were sickly sweet, strengthened by that horrible image of the dead figurehead. The golden wisps appeared out of her skin, tightening around her wrists, so tightly that Mia sobbed as she tried to wrench herself away.

'Mia, don't!' Lorin screamed. 'Stay on my back – don't let her pull you into the water!'

'She'll drag us both under!' Mia wept. 'It's revenge, Lorin. I fought against her, and now she's taking me back. She won't take you too, I won't let her.' And she slipped into the water, with the quietest of splashes. The golden threads pulled her down and a strange sense of weary peace settled in Mia's limbs. She was so tired. She could close her eyes and just let the water hold her for a while…

She had forgotten Lorin's mane, twisted around

her wrist. The dreamy laziness jolted away and she awoke, choking and cold, dragged between the golden threads and the silver ones, water and air, dream-sweetness and sharp reality.

There were figures in the water around her – not only Lorin, dragging her back to the surface, but graceful, jewel-coloured creatures, swirling around her and clawing at her golden bonds.

Mia held out her wrists to them gratefully, but their teeth and nails dug into the threads and the spell tore her skin so painfully that she screamed, and breathed in sea, and started to drown.

She broke the surface, lifted up by mermaids all around her, drowned for the third time in as many days.

'Mia, we can break the spell.' Ara shook her. 'Mia, listen! But only if you truly want it gone. All of us together here in the deep water where we're strongest, we can break the tie to your mother. But it will break something inside you too. You will no longer be hers – is that what you want?'

Mia choked, holding up her wrists, trying desperately to tell them yes. She nodded fiercely, glaring into Ara's dark eyes as the mermaid wrenched the last traces of her family out of her heart.

She felt herself go, the little child who had padded after her mama through the passages of the palace. Always quiet, always obedient, golden-haired and good. She had been bewitched all the time, she saw now. Tiny, harmless charms to shush her crying or tidy her hair, but they'd grown and stretched until they had smothered her.

That child went, sent away to follow the spell like a path, back to the woman who'd bewitched her. Mia stayed behind, no longer tied. It was oddly painless – as though it had been her mother who had hurt her, all this time, and now she was gone. But even though it didn't hurt, Mia could feel the deepness of the hole inside her, and the water, seeping slowly in to fill the emptiness. The sea, making itself a part of her and claiming her for its own.

Wearily grateful, Mia hauled herself onto Lorin's

back and the mermaids circled them, watching.

'Thank you,' she murmured. It seemed a ridiculously small and easy thing to say.

Ara smiled. 'You came after us.'

'To say goodbye.'

Ara swam closer, and Mia smiled as the sunlight glittered on her sister's red and gold and amber hair. She looked stronger and even more beautiful out here, in the deeper water. The other mermaids crowded closer too, their long, thin hands stroking at Lorin's silvery flanks and caressing Mia's torn and sodden tunic. Their skin was milky pale, as though their veins ran with saltwater, instead of blood. Their hair spilled around them in the water, all colours, like the sunlight glittering on the sea. They seemed so beautiful, and so alien, and Mia longed to slide from Lorin's back and sink down into the deep water to swim with them again.

'We should take her with us,' one of the other mermaids said, staring at Mia with cold green eyes. 'She knows us now. We can't let her go back to the city.'

For a moment, Mia's heart leapt. To swim with them, for always, just as she'd wanted! She could – Ara had shown her it could be done when she had given Mia air to breathe underwater. It would work somehow.

But Ara was shaking her head. 'Only in dreams, Mia. That spell was part of me. It was my air I gave you. I can't do it over and over – even though I wish I could.'

'We should still take her,' the green-eyed mermaid whispered.

'No!' Ara rounded on her. 'This is the child who warned us!'

'The child who brought the ships...' one of the others hissed.

Mia felt Lorin inch closer to her in the water, drawing up her haunches, as though she was preparing to leap. 'Don't,' she breathed into Lorin's white lily ear. 'We wouldn't make it. They're faster than us.'

'The child who woke the creature and *destroyed* the ships!' Ara yelled. 'We must let them go. If we take her with us, she'll drown. She's a not a sea-creature, don't you understand?'

'It doesn't matter.' The green-eyed one reached out and caught Mia's ankle, her fingers cold and strong as iron. 'We can take her.'

Mia stared into the green eyes, so much stranger and older than Ara's. 'I wish I could come with you,' she whispered. 'I wish I could see what you see, even for a moment, before my breath failed. I dreamed of it, so often.' She leant down, winding her fingers into the mermaid's white blonde hair. 'I would come with you,' she whispered. 'If I could...' She could feel Lorin tensing under her, desperate to plunge out of the circle, but Mia knew they'd never be allowed to escape.

'You'll always wish you had,' the mermaid sighed. 'You'll feel the current pulling inside you. The sea will tug at that emptiness in your heart. The tides will turn, and your blood will call to you to follow.'

'I know,' Mia said, turning to look at Ara. 'It's calling me now.'

The mermaid nodded – and then she let go, slipping back into the circle. 'Go home,' she hissed. 'Dream of us, little land girl.' And then she disappeared under the water in a flash of emerald scales. The others darted after her, leaving only Ara staring up at Mia and Lorin.

'Put the comb in your hair,' Ara said, trying to smile. 'Put the comb in your hair before you sleep, and you'll dream of us, I promise.'

'Will it be like before?' Mia begged. 'Now my mother's spell is gone, will I still swim with you in my dreams? Will it be real?'

Ara nodded, and twisted away, a golden amber shadow arrowing deep down in the water. Mia and Lorin stared after her, Mia trailing her fingers across the surface, stretching out to touch the mergirl one last time. But Ara was gone, leaving behind only the hiss of the ripples on the water singing for her, singing inside her.

'I truly hope so. Goodbye, little sister!'

'Goodbye,' Mia whispered back, pressing her face against Lorin's warm neck. 'I'll dream of you, always…'

THE END

Don't miss the next enchanting
story from Magical Venice...

The Maskmaker's daughter

Coming soon

Read on for a sneak peek...

CHAPTER ONE

Colette ran her fingers gently over the silk. She flinched a little as her roughened fingertips caught against the delicate fabric, and swiftly tucked her hands away in the folds of her skirt. The silk was too precious to risk snagging the threads, but she wanted to touch. She wanted to wrap herself in it and feel the cool blueness shining on her skin.

It shimmered so, glowing blue and green, depending on how the light fell, how it was folded, how it shifted when she ran her fingers over its gleaming surface. But she mustn't, even though she felt as though each thinner-than-hair thread was calling out to her. The tiny spells she worked with Ma jumped inside her, making her fingers tremble. They were old, worn charms, nothing grand. Just cantrips muttered against knots in the sewing silk or blunted scissors, magic that had been passed on to apprentice after apprentice, to smooth the hard life of a seamstress just a little.

There was more magic in the blue silk, Colette was sure. It was from the East, Ma said. It had come off a ship, moored up at the mouth of the Grand Canal. Ma had tried to hustle Colette away as they heard the merchant cursing, but Colette had ducked under her arm. She had seen a glimpse of that shining blue, she told Ma later, but it wasn't true. She had known it was there, inside the water-spoiled wrappings. It had called to her. They had bargained with the cloth merchant, who was glad to get something for the spoiled bale of cloth, and carried it home, lugging it along the little calles and bridges. When they'd opened it out, the great salty streaks that had so infuriated the merchant seemed to have seeped away. It was inside the cloth, Colette thought sometimes, looking at the watery dance of the sunlight on the silk.

Oh, the dresses she could make, if the fabric were really hers… It was a waste, that all its colour and life should be buried under crystal embroidery, gold thread and lace.

'Colette!' Her mother's voice broke sharply into her thoughts, and her hands jumped inside the thin cotton of her skirt. 'Colette, stop daydreaming! We don't have time. Put that silk away. Tidy your hair. They'll be here, any moment.'

'I know.' Colette jumped up, and the shot-silk spilled off her lap in a watery mass.

Her mother clucked warningly, and reached out a hand to the precious stuff. Then she leaned back against her chair, caught by a spasm of coughing.

Colette watched her worriedly, standing there with her arms full of silk and hating the way the bones of her mother's shoulders stood out.

'The dust…' her mother whispered at last. 'Only the dust. All these trimmings and scraps and threads, Colette. It all makes dust.'

'I'll sweep it up,' Colette promised eagerly. 'I didn't sweep properly yesterday, that's why you're coughing.

And I'll wash the floor, Ma. There'll be no dust left to catch in your throat then, will there?'

'They're coming.' Her mother sprang up, clutching at the back of the chair to steady herself. 'I hear them, get out to the shop, Colette, you're faster than I am. Don't keep Madam the countess waiting!'

Colette could hear them too as she hurried out of the workroom, fixing her face into a subdued grimace of welcome. Madam's page was stomping over the paving stones to hammer on the door, and she flung it open before he could damage the paintwork.

The boy glared at her, and then stood back to usher in his mistress, who was edging irritably through the narrow door. Her dress was wide enough that she had to turn sideways, and her maid was fussing over the satin. Colette didn't recognise the dress – it had come from another tailor. Ma would have sweet-talked the countess away from that heavy patterned stuff. She looked like a walking flowerbed.

'Where is your mother, child?' the countess demanded.

'I'm here, my lady.' Colette's mother hurried in,

dropping into a curtsey and tugging Colette down with her. Colette tried not to hear the faint wheeze in her mother's chest as they bowed their heads. Ma blamed the dust, or the constant damp that seeped through the stonework from the canals, or the wood fires they burned to keep the damp off the silks. It was no wonder she coughed, she kept telling Colette. She would be better in the spring. *But it's the spring now!* Colette felt the words rising up inside her, even though she couldn't bear to say them out loud. She could only hope and pray and close her eyes and pretend that Ma would get better.

If the Countess ordered a new court costume, Colette could buy the herbs to make a posset for Ma's throat. Some eggs maybe, to make a custard to slip down easy. Colette would even be glad if Countess Morezzi bought the blue shot silk, though it made her ache inside to think of the workroom without its shimmering blue-green light.

'Would Madam like to see the dolls?' Ma asked hopefully, as she struggled upright. 'We have some entirely new fashions, straight from London. Very select. Very suited to Madam's delicate colouring.'

Colette fought not to let her lips twist into a smirk. They all knew that Madam's delicate colouring came entirely out of the little pots on her dressing table, that Sofie the maid painted on her pretty blush with a rabbit's foot. The countess would be unrecognisable without her towering puffed hair and painted face. *She'd probably look like Ma*, Colette thought, bobbing another curtsey and padding backwards to the shelves to fetch the new English dolls.

The countess peered at them, fingering the fabrics as Ma twittered on about wider paniers, and Chinese painted silk, and double pleated ribbon trimming. The dolls lay limply on Colette's outstretched arms, their faces painted with foolish little rosebud smiles. The countess poked them disapprovingly and her lips twisted in a pettish little smirk. 'The same as everyone else's…' she murmured, and Colette heard her mother's tiny sigh. She was not going to order a new dress. Perhaps Sofie would pick up a pot of rouge, or some ribbons, but there was hardly any money in those. They *needed* a new commission. Ma was one of the best dressmakers in the city, but their tiny shop wasn't grand enough for most of the court nobility. And there were all the whisperings about Ma still. So few of the dressmakers in Venice were women, there was an assumption that Ma could never be as good as a proper tailor. It didn't help that Colette's father had died soon after she was born. It had taken a long time for the Tailors' Guild to accept Ma for membership.

Colette was quite sure that Countess Morezzi only came to Harriet's because they were cheap, and convenient, in that her family's palazzo was quite close by. And there was still a certain novelty in a London seamstress in Venice. The countess could be seen as fashionably eccentric, patronising such a little out-of-the-way place.

Colette wanted to plead with her, but there was no chance of that. Ma looked defeated, and tireder than ever as she took the pattern dolls from Colette and laid them gently in their places. Colette could hear her wheezing again, and she turned back to the countess, curtseying low. 'Would you wait a moment, Madam?' she murmured. 'We have some silk – very special. No one else in the city has anything like it. It would make the most fascinating dress for Carnival, my lady.'

'No one else…?' The countess looked sharply at Colette. 'And why did you not show me this before?'

'It's quite new, my lady,' Ma put in, smiling worriedly at her. 'And very dear… Perhaps only for the most special of dresses.'

Colette sensed the countess stiffen slightly. There was a faint whisper of her satin skirts against the floor, and the silver flowers embroidered on the fabric glittered. Colette stared hard at the floor, twisting her fingers behind her back. Had Ma meant to do that? To suggest that the countess couldn't afford an expensive new dress? Because either now she would storm out and tell everyone that Harriet's was out of date, shoddy and not to be trusted, or she would order that dress, with every little extra that could possibly be squeezed on to it…

Discover the rest of Collette's
spell-binding story in

Holly Webb is an internationally bestselling author, whose books have sold over two million copies worldwide. Her much-loved *Animal Stories* series is a publishing phenomenon and to date she has penned over one hundred books for children.

The Mermaid's Sister is the second book in Holly's new series set in magical Venice, which combines the things that Holly loves most: magic, historical drama and animals.

www.holly-webb.co.uk